A New Camfield Novel of Love by

BARBARA CARTLAND

Helga in Hiding

A JOVE BOOK

HELGA IN HIDING

A Jove Book/published by arrangement with
the author

PRINTING HISTORY
Jove edition/February 1986

ISBN: 0-515-08458-1

Author's Note

THE Gaiety Theatre was a London institution and the Gaiety Girls were unique over the whole world. Lovely as goddesses, they floated to the theatre borne as it were, on immortal sandals, whether they rolled up in hansom cabs, came in their own private broughams, or were escorted by gentlemen with tail coats, top hats and white ties.

As they passed they left a glimpse of grace and beauty and a fragrance of femininity which the world does not know today.

There were all classes in their ranks, some from what was almost the gutter and some from the aristocracy, but each one had the polish and stamp of the Gaiety.

They were selected by George Edwardes, who was the best judge of female charm the world has ever known, just as he was the best judge of talent. He was the supreme manager of his time and his name on the bill of a play was the equivalent of a hallmark of quality.

Nobody since George Edwardes's days has meant what he did, and one name only since his time has stood for something like the same thing in the minds of the public, and that was C. B. Cochran.

The Gaiety shows shone and glittered and all London flocked to them. They gave London its lighter moments, its laughter, and its glorious girls.

It is difficult now for us to realise, when everything has become so dull and mundane, what these beautiful, exotic women meant to the men who watched them from the stalls and prayed they would be lucky enough to take them out to supper.

The Gaiety Girls were all beautiful, wonderful women but they not only had charm and glamour, but many of them had genuine talent as well.

chapter one

1891

MILLICENT Melrose sat in front of the mirror in her Dressing Room at the Gaiety Theatre and wondered how it was possible to feel so tired.

She had come to the Theatre early, as she always did, because it gave her a chance to be quiet before the Show, and also, she knew, to pull herself together.

Ever since she had lost Christofer it had become increasingly difficult to keep up the facade of being a star, not only before the public but also in front of those with whom she worked.

She was well aware that it was fatally easy to slip into being a nonentity and to find herself after all the years of success out of work.

It was traditional for people to say:

"I could not imagine the Gaiety without you, Milly."

But she was quite certain they would be the first to

say she was "past it," and showing her age.

The mere thought of age made her glance at herself nervously in the mirror, looking for the lines which she was sure were beginning to form round her eyes and at the corners of her mouth.

"Thirty-nine next birthday!"

It seemed as if even the flowers in the room screamed it at her, and it was like a dark cloud hanging over her head.

None of it would have mattered if Christofer was alive, but he was dead and could not help her now.

At night when she cried into her pillow she wished that she had died too.

It was true he had been twenty years older than she was, and she might have expected him to die before her, even in those far-off days when they had both been carefree and so certain that neither of them would ever grow old.

Even now she could hear, as if it were yesterday, him saying to her:

"Come away with me, my darling. I cannot live without you! I know it will cause a scandal, but my wife will divorce me, and when we are married it will all be forgotten and the social world will accept you again."

It had all sounded so plausible, with Christofer kissing her so that she thrilled with a rapture she had not believed possible.

When Christofer told her how blissfully happy they would be, it was impossible to be cautious, sensible, or to think of anything but him.

She remembered how exciting it had been when leaving a note for her father and mother she had crept out of the house one night after she was supposed to have gone to bed, and Christofer had been waiting for her at the end of the drive.

He had helped her into a closed carriage and they had driven off to what she believed would be a Heaven on earth with no regrets.

"How young I was," Milly said to herself now, "and how foolish."

And yet she knew that if she could put back the clock she would do the same thing all over again, because Christofer had been irresistible and she would have had to be made of stone to be able to refuse him.

She could still remember the little Hotel where they had stayed the night and the ecstasies they had evoked in each other, so that Christofer had said hoarsely:

"How could we fight against a love as great as ours? How could we contemplate life without each other?"

He had been so confident and so had she, when they settled in a small Manor House in an obscure village in Gloucestershire, and they both believed it was only a question of time before they were legally Lord and Lady Forsythe.

But Christofer's wife was made of sterner stuff, and when he asked her for a divorce she refused categorically, saying:

"I am your wife, and your place is with me. When you are ready to return, your home is waiting for you."

"It is ridiculous!" Christofer had raged. "She will change her mind—of course she will! It is only a question of waiting."

The difficulty while they were waiting was how they were to live.

Lord Forsythe had very little money of his own, and

3

the Trustees of his wife, who was a comparatively wealthy woman, had made sure that, while he had the handling of her income, it was impossible for him to touch the capital.

Not very intelligent over money, he found he was committed to keeping up the running expenses of the house in which his wife lived and which as she had truly said was his home.

It left him very little indeed to expend on Milly.

They struggled in the country for nearly a year, then moved to London.

"I think perhaps I had better find something to do," Milly said a little nervously.

To her surprise Christofer did not immediately refuse to discuss such an idea.

It took time—time during which they worried frantically as to how they could go on, how their bills could be met, how Christofer could somehow extract more money from his wife.

Then finally they succumbed to the inevitable and Christofer returned to see what he could do about it.

What this entailed was that to all intents and purposes he became once again a married man, appearing at social functions with his wife and, as many men have done before him, keeping a mistress on the side.

It was Milly who suffered; of course she did.

The Staffords, who were extremely respectable and had played their part in the history of England, had cut her off with the proverbial shilling, and although she might have crawled back to beg their forgiveness, she was too proud to do so.

In desperation Christofer introduced her to George

Edwardes, and one look decided the most astute Show-man of the age that she was just what he wanted at the Gaiety Theatre.

The Gaiety Girls were renowned for being quite different from ordinary Show girls.

In the first place, a number of them were well-educated and besides being beautiful they behaved like Ladies, and had in consequence a glamour that made them outstanding on the stage and sought after by every Man-about-Town who was proud to be seen in their company.

The applause, the acclamation of her beauty, and the compliments she received did a great deal to assuage Milly's feeling of guilt towards her family.

She of course did not use her real name but called herself "Millicent Melrose," and hoped that her relatives would never know what she was doing.

But whether they knew or not she had no idea, since she had no communication with them.

From the moment she became a Gaiety Girl life was far easier than it had been before.

Not only was she earning money for herself, but because Christofer played his part at home as skillfully as she played hers on the stage, his wife became more generous and he had more money to spend.

He set Milly up in a very comfortable flat in a quiet Square not far from the Gaiety Theatre and spent every moment he possibly could with her.

This usually meant he was in London mostly during the week and returned home at weekends to entertain on his estate, with shooting and hunting parties in the winter, and in the summer there was tennis, archery, and boating on the lake.

Milly tried not to think of what he was doing when he was not with her.

She was often lonely, but she told herself it was the price she had to pay for being so blissfully happy when they were together.

Of course she was approached by other men. She was too beautiful for there not to be a constant flow of flowers and invitations to supper which made Christofer jealous.

But it meant nothing to her except that her admirers filled in the hours when he was not there.

There was one man in particular who was very persistent and had pursued her now for nearly six years.

Sir Emanuel Stiener was exceedingly rich, and most of the Gaiety Girls were only too eager to accept his invitations and his presents, which were always very generous.

They fell over themselves to ingratiate themselves with a millionaire who because of his astuteness in business was known to be a friend of the Prince of Wales.

It was perhaps Milly's indifference which made him all the more determined that sooner or later she would be his.

It was of Sir Emanuel Stiener that Milly was thinking now as her eyes fell on a large basket of expensive orchids.

She was well aware that he was waiting impatiently but cleverly for her to get over the shock of Christofer's death before he approached her, as he had before, with suggestions of what a difference he could make in her life.

"I will cover you with diamonds, wrap you in sables,

6

and cosset you against everything that might distress or hurt you," he had promised.

She laughed at him and replied:

"You know I have everything I want, not diamonds, nor sables, but Christofer!"

Sir Emanuel had made no reply but looked at her with his shrewd eyes, and she thought now that perhaps he had known clairvoyantly that the sands were running out and the days of her happiness were numbered.

When she had read in the newspapers that Lord Forsythe had suffered a stroke while a guest at Marlborough House, she had been frantic with anxiety.

It was impossible for her personally to make enquiries at Forsythe House in Park Lane as to how he was, but she persuaded a half dozen of her admirers to do so on her behalf.

All they were told was that he was very gravely ill, but there was still hope for his recovery.

Of course there was no question of Milly being allowed to see him, and she could only wait and know as the days passed that it was inevitable he would die.

Actually it was her work on the stage that helped her over the shock better than if she had been a lady of leisure with nothing to do but sit at home and weep.

"The Show must go on!" was the old troupers' cry, and Milly played her part automatically.

She had by now become an institution in the Shows produced by George Edwardes.

She had been promoted to having small parts in the main cast, and because her voice was soft and cultured and her diction clear she eventually always had one sketch in which she was the principal.

She was well aware that this would not last for ever, and when she thought of the future there seemed only one end to it, and that was with Sir Emanuel.

At first she had felt that if another man even touched her hand she would scream with the horror of it, but Sir Emanuel was far too clever to put pressure on her or to impose himself physically upon her.

Instead, he sent her flowers, notes of sympathy which were very eloquent, and expensive but practical presents like a case of champagne or a pot of *pâté de foie gras* or caviar.

She wondered if she should send them back to him, then knew it was something she dared not do.

"I hate him!" she told herself a million times.

But she knew the hatred was because he was alive while Christofer was dead.

"Dead!"

The word seemed almost to echo round her Dressing Room and she put out her hand, aware it was shaking a little, for the bottle of brandy which was concealed behind a large photograph of herself at the end of the dressing table.

She poured about two tablespoonfuls into a glass and stared at it as she put down the bottle, knowing that Christofer would have been angry with her for giving in to what was inevitably the actor's panacea of Dutch courage.

"I cannot manage without it, darling," she said to him pathetically.

Her brain was telling her that she had said the same thing every night for the last two weeks, and the brandy bottle had been replaced more times than she cared to count.

"I cannot go on like this!" she said aloud.

Even as she spoke she lifted the glass to her lips and felt the fiery liquid slipping down her throat, sweeping away a little of her overwhelming fatigue.

She drank again and as she did so there was a knock on the door.

"Who is it?" she asked, slipping the glass as she spoke behind another photograph of herself, wearing a spectacular gown.

"There's a lidy ter see yer, Miss Melrose!"

It was Joe the doorkeeper who spoke, and Milly was just about to say that she had no wish to receive visitors, when the door opened and somebody came into the dressing room.

Milly looked at her without interest.

It was a young woman who she supposed must be a fan, and she could not understand how Joe had been so absurd as to let one of the autograph hunters who were always outside the stage door come up to her Dressing Room.

Then the girl in the doorway said:

"You are just as beautiful as I thought you would be, Aunt Millicent! And I am so excited to meet you in real life!"

As the girl spoke she came nearer to Milly, who stared at her in sheer astonishment.

"Who are you?" she asked.

"I am your niece, Helga Wensley, and you must please forgive me for coming to you so unexpectedly, but Mama told me what I was to do before . . . she died."

There was a little tremor in the girl's voice and Milly saw the tears come into her eyes, very beautiful eyes that seemed to fill her small, pointed face.

"Are you telling me," Milly asked, "that you are my sister Beryl's daughter, and that she is dead?"

The girl nodded as if for a moment it were impossible to speak. Then she said:

"Mama died four days ago. She was buried yesterday. I have come here to ask you to help me . . . as she was sure you would do."

Milly put her hand up to her forehead.

"I can hardly believe what you are telling me," she said, "or that Beryl could be—dead."

"She has been ill with consumption for the last two years," Helga replied, "and as she grew weaker . . . and weaker there was nothing the doctors could do to . . . help her."

Now the tears were running down the girl's face, and as if Milly realised it was up to her to take control of the situation, she said:

"Sit down, child, and tell me about it. But I cannot see how I can possibly help you, and I am sure there are many people to look after you, even though your mother is not there."

"That is . . . not so," Helga said. "Please . . . may I tell you . . . everything?"

"That is what I want you to do," Milly replied.

There was an empty chair beside the dressing table on which Helga sat down, and as she did so Milly realised how lovely she was, looking very like her mother when she was a young girl.

10

Milly guessed that Helga must be about the same age as she had been when she first met Christofer.

"How old are you?" she asked curiously.

"I am eighteen," Helga replied.

That was what Milly had thought she would be, and she remembered that Beryl, who was two years older than herself, had married Lord Wensley six months after she had run away with Christofer.

She had read every mention of it she could find in the social columns of the newspapers, and she had wondered if Beryl, despite being shocked at the way she had left home, had missed her amongst her bride's-maids.

Then after the wedding she had heard no more about her sister, and sometimes when she was alone she had longed to be able to gossip with her as they had done when they were girls.

She could see a great resemblance in Helga's face to her mother's, but she thought with a little pang that the girl was more beautiful.

Beautiful in a young, springlike manner which she herself had lost years ago, but which when she was behind the footlights she still tried to recapture even though now it was only an illusion.

"I have come to you, Aunt Millicent," Helga was saying, "because Mama told me to, and I am also desperate!"

"Why should you be desperate?" Milly asked. "I do not understand."

"I . . . I do not expect you would know that Papa . . . died five years ago?"

"I had no idea of it!" Milly answered. "There seemed to be very little about your mother in the newspapers, and I had no other way of learning what she was doing."

"There was nothing in the newspapers because there was nothing to write about," Helga said. "We were very, very poor before Papa died and we lived in a small house in the country where Papa bred horses, and although we were very happy he used to worry because they brought him in so little money."

"I always imagined your mother would be well off," Milly said. "What happened?"

Helga made a helpless little gesture with her hand which Milly noticed was very graceful.

"I think Papa lost a lot of money on the Stock Exchange, and although Mama had a small allowance from Grandpapa, he also was not very rich, and I think Uncle Richard was extravagant."

Milly smiled.

Although her brother was younger than she, she was quite certain that when he grew up he would be like a great number of their Stafford ancestors.

Although they might be brave in battle, they were also dashing in peacetime, gambling away their money or spending it on expensive horses and attractive women.

"Anyway," Helga continued, "when Papa died, Mama had no idea how we could make ends meet. We sold off the horses, but we did not get very much for them, and when that money had gone Mama was beginning to think that we should have to beg Uncle Richard, who was now the head of the family to keep us, when Sir Hector Preston came along."

"Who was he?" Milly asked.

"I suppose you would describe him as a fox-hunting Squire!" Helga said with a little flash of humour.

"You did not like him?"

"He was a red-faced, bullying type of man, but he fell in love with Mama and asked her to marry him. Although she really had no wish to accept him, it seemed the only solution to our difficulties."

"So your mother became Lady Preston," Milly said as if she were getting it clear in her own mind.

Helga nodded.

"We moved into his big, ugly house in Worcestershire where my stepfather was Master of Hounds, and considered to be quite an important personage in his own way."

"Was your mother happy?" Milly enquired.

"She missed Papa desperately," Helga replied, "and she never really cared for my stepfather's friends. They thought of nothing but horses, they drank a lot, and when they came to the house were very noisy and so different in every way from Papa."

"I know what you mean," Milly said. "Go on. What happened?"

"Mama seemed to grow quieter and at the same time thinner and more fragile," Helga said. "She did not see a doctor, but I thought sometimes she was in pain and she always seemed tired. Then suddenly a year ago she said to me:

"'I am going to die, Helga, and I do not know what will become of you when I do.'

"'You must not die, Mama!' I cried. 'How could I possibly manage without you? It would be horrible here alone!'

"'I have been thinking about that,' Mama said, 'and I am worried, very worried, Helga!'

13

"She paused for a moment and I thought she was making up her mind whether or not to tell me what was frightening her. Then she said:

"'I do not like the type of men who come to this house or the way they look at you, and they are certainly not gentlemen like your father, or the sort of man I would want you to marry.'

"'No, of course not, Mama!' I said quickly.

"'That is why,' Mama went on, 'we have to decide what you should do when I die, and who you should go to.'

"I thought for a moment, then I said:

"'I suppose, although he might not really wish to, Uncle Richard will have me.'

"Mama was silent for a moment before she said:

"'Your stepfather will be your Guardian and I have the idea he would stop you from going to your uncle, even if you wanted to do so.'

"'Why? Why should he do that?' I asked.

"'Because, dearest, he is jealous of Uncle Richard and also thinks he should pay more attention to us.'

"Mama paused before she said in a low voice as if she were afraid of being overheard:

"'If you want the truth and it is only right that you should know: Uncle Richard has said that he does not like your stepfather and has no wish to entertain us, or in fact to see us again!'

"I wondered about that," Helga said, "and I guessed there must have been a row of some sort, although I had not been told about it."

"It certainly sounds like it," Milly said. "What did your mother suggest you should do?"

"She said to me:

"'That leaves me with only one relation, my darling, and it is somebody you have never met.'

"I must have looked puzzled," Helga said, "because she added:

"'It is your Aunt Millicent, my sister, who as you have been told ran away from home and has become a famous figure on the stage.'"

Helga smiled and it seemed to illuminate her face.

"Of course I knew about you, Aunt Millicent. I always thought it was a thrilling story, how you had left Grandpapa's house in the middle of the night, and having run away became one of the beautiful Gaiety Girls."

"I am surprised you have heard about me," Milly said, "because I changed my name, and I thought no one would ever know."

"But everybody knew!" Helga answered. "My Nanny used to talk about you in a whisper, and Mama used to talk about you to Papa. She used to point out pictures of you in the *Ladies Journal* or one of the other magazines, and although she did not show them to me I used to find them as soon as she went out, and read everything about you."

"I had no idea..." Milly murmured.

"You looked so lovely in every picture," Helga went on enthusiastically, "and I longed to meet you and be able to boast about you to my friends. But Mama said I was not to tell anybody outside the house who you were."

"And yet your mother, before she died, told you to come to me!" Milly said in a surprised voice.

Helga looked away from her as she said:

"It is... difficult to... tell you what h-happened."

15

"Nevertheless I want to know!" Milly said quickly.

"My stepfather had never liked me," Helga said frankly. "I think actually he was angry that Mama did not give him the son he wanted and he resented it when she showed any affection for me."

Helga's voice broke as she went on:

"He used to . . . beat me . . . whenever I did anything wrong . . . and often . . . I think . . . just because he hated me for being there in the house with them."

Milly drew in her breath, but she did not interrupt as Helga continued:

"It was when Mama was so ill that he began to look at me in a . . . way that made me afraid . . . then one day . . . I found out what he was planning."

"What was that?" Milly asked.

"It was about ten days before Mama died," Helga said. "I was reading in the Library, thinking he was out of the house, when I heard him come along the passage talking to somebody."

She paused for a moment before she went on:

"Without really thinking, I hid in a cupboard where a lot of old maps and books were kept. I suppose it was a silly thing to do, but I did it instinctively because I always avoided Steppapa whenever it was possible.

"I left the door slightly ajar so that I could breathe and I knew the man he was with whose voice I recognised was Bernard Howell. He was one of his closest friends who was always coming either to luncheon or dinner, and whom I hated because I thought he was cruel to his horses."

"What do you mean—cruel?" Milly asked.

"He used his whip at the slightest provocation and

16

spurred them too hard. I even heard the servants say when they thought I was not listening that because he was so cruel to his wife she committed suicide!"

Milly gave a little gasp, but she merely said impatiently:

"Go on!"

"First my stepfather poured out whisky for both of them," Helga continued, "then as they sat down in the big leather armchairs, Mr. Howell said:

"'How is your wife?'

"'Worse,' my stepfather said. 'It is only a question of days!'"

There was silence. Then Mr. Howell asked:

"'And when she dies, what do you intend to do about Helga?'

"'What do you want me to do?'

"'You know the answer to that, but your wife would never entertain such an idea.'

"'As far as I am concerned,' my stepfather said, 'you can have her, and the quicker the better! She irritates me. She always has!'

"'I know that,' Mr. Howell said. 'I will be glad to take her off your hands, and as she will be in mourning it will be a good excuse for a quiet wedding in a Registry Office.'

"'Then arrange it,' Steppapa said, 'and I wish you joy of her! She is an obstinate little brat! I have never been able to prevent her from defying me.'

"Bernard Howell laughed and it was a very unpleasant sound.

"'She will find it a painful thing to do as far as I am concerned,' he said. 'I know exactly how to treat unbroken fillies whether they are horses or women!'

"I heard Steppapa put down his glass," Helga said, "and he rose to his feet, saying:

"'Well, that is arranged. That was all I wanted to see you about.'

"They walked towards the door and when I heard them leave I knew with a terror that made me want to scream that I had to run away."

There was a note of fear in Helga's voice that Milly did not miss. Then she said slowly, as if she were trying to collect her thoughts:

"I can understand what you are feeling, Helga, but you are quite sure it would be as bad as that? After all, if this Mr. Howell wants to marry you, it means you will at least have a roof over your head, and someone to look after you."

"I would rather die than marry him!" Helga said passionately. "He is horrible, cruel, evil! I can feel it vibrating from him when he comes near me."

She gave a little sob and clasped her hands together as she said:

"Please ... Aunt Millicent ... help me. I will scrub floors, do anything ... anything rather than have to ... marry a man like that!"

There was only a small silence before Milly said understandingly:

"Of course I will help you, but it is very difficult to know how to do so."

As she spoke she was thinking of how desperately poor she was herself and how many bills had accumulated since Christofer's death.

Her rent was overdue, she owed money to a number

of shops, and although the solution was staring her in the face in the shape of Sir Emanuel, she had hoped against hope that by a miracle something would turn up.

"I would not wish to be an . . . encumbrance," Helga was saying humbly, "but I feel sure there must be some way I can earn my living. After all, however poor we were, Mama saw that I was well-educated."

"I am sure she did," Milly said absentmindedly. "But what can you do?"

"I can play the piano . . . but not well enough to be professional," Helga said. "I can sew, although it is not something I particularly enjoy. I can ride, and I can tell fortunes!"

"Tell fortunes?" Milly echoed in astonishment. "How can you do that?"

Helga laughed and it was a very attractive sound.

"It all started when my Nanny used to try to tell fortunes by the tea leaves," she explained, "but what she said was usually wrong, and I used to correct her and whatever I said came true! That meant that the other servants used to consult me and so did the people in the village, although Mama said it was a lot of nonsense, and I was not to encourage them."

"It seems extraordinary!" Milly enquired.

"I think a lot of it was really coincidence," Helga said frankly. "Then one year when they were arranging the Church Fête the Vicar asked Mama if, to raise money for the Church I would dress up as a Gypsy and tell people's fortunes for a shilling a time."

"And your mother let you?"

"She said she could hardly refuse, as it was all in a good cause. If people were ready to believe such a lot of Fairy Stories, there was no reason why the Church should not benefit from it."

"What happened?"

"Everybody in the village said that everything I told them came true. In fact, one girl whom I had warned not to ride, however much she was tempted to do so, disobeyed me."

Milly was listening intently as Helga went on:

"She had an accident and her leg was broken so badly that it had to be amputated! After that people said I was a Witch!"

"I am not surprised!" Milly said. "It certainly sounds very creepy!"

"It rather frightens me," Helga admitted, "but I cannot help seeing things that are going to happen. Not always but when I concentrate on somebody, then, good or bad, I see the truth."

"Well, you certainly cannot become a Fortune-Teller in London!" Milly said quickly. "What we have to decide together is . . ."

There was a knock on the door that interrupted her.

"What is it?" she asked sharply.

"A gentleman to see you, Miss, an' he says it's very important!"

"I cannot see anybody, Joe!" Milly replied.

"It's the Duke of Rocklington, Miss, an' he won't take no for an answer!"

Milly gave a little gasp and looked around wildly, as if for a moment she could not believe what the Dressing Room looked like.

Then aloud she said:

"Wait one minute, Joe, until I am decent."

As she spoke she rose to her feet and beckoned Helga towards where across a corner of the Dressing Room was hung a curtain behind which she changed when there were people in the other part of the room.

Now as she pulled the curtain aside and pushed Helga behind it she whispered:

"Do not make a sound!"

As Helga disappeared she pulled the curtain back into place and put a hard chair in front of it.

Then she sat in the chair she had just vacated, and taking her glass from behind the photograph she finished off what remained in it before she called out:

"Ask His Grace to come in, Joe!"

A moment later the door opened and the Duke of Rocklington came into the Dressing Room, seeming to fill it with his presence.

He was a tall, broad-shouldered man and exceedingly good-looking.

There was no one in London who did not know the Duke, and certainly no one in the Theatre World.

It was no secret that he had invested a great deal of money in George Edwardes's productions, and a word from His Grace could either make or break an aspiring young actress.

Milly had of course known the Duke for years and had often attended the supper parties he gave at Romano's and occasionally in his own house.

But he had never been in her Dressing Room, except when there was a party in progress, and now she wondered frantically whether he was perhaps the conveyor of bad news that her services were no longer required.

She was well aware that, although she had tried not

21

to let her personal feelings intrude, the performances she had given since Christofer died were inferior to those she had given before.

She felt as if she carried a heavy stone in her chest and had been numbed by a shock which seemed to have paralysed not only her body, but also her brain.

She had struggled on, but she knew the Duke expected perfection and would undoubtedly be the first to realise that she was not up to form.

She was however actress enough to smile at him beguilingly.

It was the same smile that had sold thousands of postcards of her in every Stationer's shop all over London, and which ensured that there was still a large contingent of autograph-hunters to besiege her every time she went in or out of the stage door.

"This is a surprise, Your Grace!" she said, holding out her hand with a gesture that was almost royal.

"Good evening, Milly!"

The Duke kissed her hand, foreign fashion, his lips not actually touching her skin.

Then he pulled up a chair from the other side of the room and sitting down beside her said:

"I want your help!"

"My help?" Milly exclaimed, thinking this was the second time her help had been asked that evening, and both times it had been exceedingly surprising.

"How can I possibly help Your Grace?" she asked before the Duke could speak. "I should have thought the 'boot was very much on the other foot' and it is something I might be asking you."

"The help I require is something which I think it is

possible only for you to give me," the Duke said, "and that is why I have come to the Theatre early, when I knew you would be alone, to ask your assistance."

"You are certainly making me very curious!" Milly said lightly.

To her surprise the Duke looked serious, and putting his tall hat and cane down on the dressing table, he seemed for a moment to have difficulty in finding words in which to express himself.

A dozen ideas meanwhile flashed through Milly's mind as to what he could possibly want of her, none of which had any likelihood of being the truth, and she could only wait, thinking that when one strange and rather unexpected thing happened, there was usually another to follow it.

But never in her wildest dreams had she expected the Duke of Rocklington to approach her in such a way.

She knew a great deal about him. He was enormously rich and the most sought-after bachelor in the whole of the Social World.

He had made it very clear that he had no intention of marrying and preferred when he was not in attendance upon the Prince of Wales to be in the company of the latest and most beautiful actress the Theatre World could provide.

At least a half dozen Gaiety Girls had passed through his hands in the last two years, and although they extolled his attractions even after being discarded and were apparently still enamoured of him he had no further use for them.

He was certainly a phenomenon in that way, and looking at his broad forehead, his dark flashing eyes, and the squareness of his chin, Milly could understand any young woman being bowled over by his attractions, without counting the importance of his being a Duke and the fact that he was extremely generous.

But she knew also that he was a force to be reckoned with.

There were stories of how he and George Edwardes had fallen out on numerous occasions.

The Duke had always won, and it was said that George Edwardes had always conceded that in this, if in nothing else, the Duke was the "Guv'nor" and not himself.

There was a curve on his lips which Milly knew would be extremely sarcastic and at times cynical, and she was aware that he was capable of making a woman very unhappy if she really loved him in the same way as she had loved Christofer.

There were, of course, stories of Ladies with broken hearts, who lived not among the brilliant lights of the Theatre, but in the Duke's Social World.

It was easy to understand that if a woman aspired to marry him, but found it was something he had no intention of offering her, she could in consequence find it agonising to lose him.

It all flashed through Milly's mind until the Duke had settled himself back in his chair and said:

"Now, Milly, listen to my problem, and find me a solution to it!"

chapter two

"I have been negotiating," the Duke began, "a financial deal on a very large scale with an American, and not only am I concerned but also, and of course this is confidential, is the Prince of Wales."

Milly made a little murmur, but she did not interrupt.

She knew the Prince was always hard up and that quite a number of financial geniuses as well as his personal friends helped him financially from time to time.

"Everything has gone smoothly," the Duke continued, "and Cyrus Vanderfeld is due to arrive in England tomorrow and is coming to stay with me at Rock for the weekend."

It flashed through Milly's mind that perhaps he was going to invite her as one of his guests, although it seemed extraordinary that he should do so.

"I have learnt at the very last moment," the Duke went on, "that Mr. Vanderfeld is bringing with him his daughter. But someone who has been helping me with the negotiations in America tells me that he is determined and in fact obsessed with the idea of his daughter becoming the Duchess of Rocklington!"

The Duke spoke with a hard note in his voice while Milly straightened herself and stared at him in surprise.

"But, surely, an American . . . ?" she began.

"I have no intention of marrying anybody," the Duke interrupted, "and certainly not an American who would not understand the English way of life."

"Then what is your problem?" Milly asked.

"It is quite simple," the Duke replied. "I have no wish to offend Mr. Vanderfeld at this particular moment. In fact, it is extremely important that I keep him agreeable and pleasant until the contract is signed. But if, as my friend tells me, he is set on his daughter becoming a Duchess, then I have to tread carefully."

"What can you do?"

"The answer to that is up to you," the Duke replied.

"To me?"

"What I want you to find me," the Duke said slowly, "is a young actress who will play the part of my *fiancée* for as long as Mr. Vanderfeld remains in England."

Now Milly understood what she was being asked to do and her first thought was that it would not be easy to find the type of young actress the Duke required.

"It should not be too difficult," the Duke said as if he had read her thoughts. "Surely there must be, somewhere in London, a young woman who was like yourself when you first dazzled the Theatrical World?"

26

He smiled and it made him look very attractive as he said:

"You know exactly what I am saying, Milly. She must look like a Lady, behave like a Lady and, if possible, be one!"

Milly did not laugh as he expected; instead, she looked worried.

"It is not easy, Your Grace," she said. "As you doubtless know, I ran away from home because I was in love with Christofer Forsythe. I went on the stage only when we were both so hard up that we had no idea where our next penny was coming from."

"And so the Gaiety gained a star," the Duke said, "for which we are all very grateful."

Milly thanked him with a smile for the compliment, then she said:

"As Your Grace knows, there are numerous young and very pretty young actresses, both here at the Gaiety and at other Theatres, but I cannot think of one who is the type you require and would not seem, even to an American, ill at ease in the *rôle* of your future wife."

"That is nonsense!" the Duke said sharply. "There must be somebody! God knows, enough girls flock to London to act. All I am asking is that one of them should act for a more exclusive and smaller audience than she is doing at the moment."

"Who else will be in the party?" Milly asked unexpectedly.

"A number of my friends," the Duke replied, "the majority of them of some Social importance since I understand that Mr. Vanderfeld is very much impressed by the English aristocracy."

Milly made a little gesture with her hands.

"In that case they would very soon know, even if Mr. Vanderfeld did not, that your supposed *fiancée* was a fake. Unless of course you let them into the secret."

"No, certainly not!" the Duke ejaculated. "I am not as foolish as that! It would be too good a joke not to be repeated and re-repeated in every Club in St. James's and sooner or later Vanderfeld would learn that he had been taken for a ride."

"I see your point," Milly said, "but that makes it even more difficult."

"Oh, come on, Milly," the Duke said, "you are the only person I know who is really qualified to help me. Surely there must be some young girl who would 'pass muster'?"

"I cannot think of one," Milly said unhappily.

"I do not believe you!" the Duke said sharply as though he thought she was deliberately obstructing him. "By the way, I forgot to say that whoever played the part for me would be very well rewarded for doing so."

He hesitated for a moment before he said:

"Shall we make the offer a really tempting one? I suggest I pay the principal in the drama a thousand pounds, and give you a thousand for finding her, coaching her, and seeing that she is properly dressed."

Milly gave a little gasp.

One thousand pounds seemed an incredible amount of money.

Immediately it flashed through her mind that for the moment it would solve her problems and she need no longer feel that her only salvation lay with Sir Emanuel.

"It is too much!" she murmured without really meaning it.

"Not if you give me what I want," the Duke said. "There is too much at stake to quibble over trifles."

Milly was tempted to retort that a thousand pounds was far from a trifle to her, or indeed to any young actress who was struggling to keep alive on the small salary which would be all she was receiving.

But she thought it would be a mistake to argue with the Duke, and instead, she tried to think frantically of any girl she had noticed lately in the Theatre.

She was uncomfortably aware that although they were extremely pretty and had exactly the right figures that were expected of them in their profession, the minute they opened their mouths they gave away their origins only too blatantly.

At the same time 1000 pounds!

The sun seemed to dance in front of her eyes, and she knew the Duke was aware of it and watching her closely.

"I must think," she murmured.

At that moment there was a knock on the door.

"Five minutes, Miss Melrose!" a voice said warningly, and as he spoke the door opened and Milly's Dresser came into the room.

The Duke then rose to his feet.

"I will come back to talk to you in the interval," he said. "I am relying on you, Milly, and if you can help me, you know I will always be very grateful."

Milly felt there was a warning in the words and it was almost as if he added: If you do not . . .

She did not need to end the sentence.

Then as the Duke left the Dressing Room a small voice from behind the curtain asked:

"May I come out now, Aunt Millicent?"

Milly started.

She had been so intent on what the Duke was saying that she had, although it seemed extraordinary, forgotten for the moment that Helga was there.

Now as she came back into the Dressing Room there was a light in her eyes, and before she could speak Milly knew what she was going to say.

"A thousand pounds, Aunt Millicent!" she whispered. "I could play that part!"

"No, no, of course not!" Milly said quickly. "Your mother would be horrified at your being mixed up in such a way with the Duke!"

"Why? He sounds rather nice."

"Too many women have thought that in the past!" Milly snapped.

Then as her Dresser, who had been collecting a large flower-covered hat from a corner of the room, brought it to her, Milly said:

"This is my niece, Annie, but no one is to know that, except you, and no one is to come in here and meet her while I am on stage. Do you understand?"

"I 'ears you," Annie said pertly, and smiling at Helga she said: "'Ow-de-do, Miss? Is this the first time you've bin to the Theatre?"

"The very first time," Helga answered, "and please, could I see the Show? I do want to see you on stage, Aunt Millicent."

"You are to stay here," Milly said sharply. "You know

as well as I do that you cannot sit in the auditorium alone with no one to look after you."

Helga's face fell and Annie said:

"I'll take her along for a peep from the wings. Nobody'll see 'er there, an' I'll bring her back before you 'as to change."

"All right," Milly agreed reluctantly, "but I do not wish anybody to know who she is. And while you are in the theatre, Helga, you call me 'Miss Melrose.'"

"Yes, of course," Helga agreed.

There was another loud knock on the door.

"Three minutes, Miss Melrose. They're expecting you on stage!"

"I am coming!" Milly said.

She would have liked another sip of brandy but thought it would be a mistake to drink in front of Helga.

She had not missed the wide-eyed admiration in the girl's eyes which she found rather touching.

It was extraordinary, after years of knowing how violently her family disapproved of her and how they had brushed her out of their lives as if she were something unclean, that her niece should look at her in the adoring manner that she was used to from her fans who sat in the Gallery.

"I must go," Milly said, "and do not forget what I told you."

"No, of course not, Au—Miss Melrose!" Helga replied.

But by this time with her silk skirt swishing around her ankles and her head held high balancing a huge concoction of flowers and feathers, Milly was halfway down the corridor.

31

"Now sit down and be comfortable, Miss," Annie said. "Your aunt won't be away for long, and it'll be at least half an hour before I can take you down to the wings."

"It is very kind of you to take the trouble," Helga said.

"I knows what you're feeling," Annie said. "When you first come to the Gaiety it's like stepping into Fairyland, but after a bit you see the snags and pitfalls and it ain't half as pretty as it looks."

"All the same, it is very exciting!" Helga said.

She sat chatting to Annie until Milly returned, looking rather tired, and as Milly took off her hat she automatically reached for the bottle behind the photograph.

"You'd better change your gown first," Annie said.

This was another concoction of tulle and sequins, of diamonds and flowers, held up with velvet ribbon, to wear in a scene in which each girl was more beautiful than the last.

Helga could only sit enthralled, appreciating the pure silk stockings that covered her aunt's shapely legs, and her underclothes trimmed with real lace, which George Edwardes insisted on his girls wearing.

"It is details that count," he often said.

And it was details that made his Shows unique, and his women the most admired and captivating in the world.

When Annie had finished doing up Milly's gown at the back, she said:

"Will you wait outside for a moment, Annie? I want to talk to my niece."

"It's unusual for you to have secrets," Annie said tartly, but she went from the Dressing Room, closing the door behind her.

"Now listen, Helga," Milly said. "I know you think it is unkind of me not to let you play the part the Duke is asking, but you have no idea what it entails."

"Mama has often explained to me what the parties were like in the big houses, and how much she enjoyed them when she was young," Helga replied.

"We both enjoyed them," Milly said, "but when we went to stay in the 'Big Houses,' as you call them, our mother accompanied us. We were so strictly chaperoned and looked after that there was no question of our finding ourselves in any unpleasant or difficult situation."

"Why should there be an unpleasant or difficult situation in the Duke's house?" Helga asked.

Milly hesitated for a moment. Then she told her the truth.

"Because, my dear child, you will be playing the part of a Lady, but the Duke will believe you to be an actress, and the two are very different things."

"But he will treat me as he would if I were really his *fiancée*," Helga said, "and as if I were a Lady."

Milly thought her niece had brains.

At the same time, she could have no idea of the Duke's character and reputation, or of the number of his love affairs that were talked about and counted in the same way as a sportsman counted the birds he shot.

"I would not entertain the idea," she said aloud, "so there is no use talking about it, Helga. If I am to look

33

after you, I have to do it in the way your mother would have done, and that certainly does not include allowing you to be a guest of the Duke of Rocklington!"

"I think Mama would have been rather pleased if I was invited to a house party consisting of a number of Ladies and Gentlemen," Helga said. "She hated the type of man my stepfather entertained, and thought they were ill-bred and behaved in what she called a 'common' way which made her wince."

Milly did not answer and after a moment Helga said:

"You cannot really mean me to miss the chance of earning a thousand pounds, Aunt Millicent? There would be no need then for me to worry about working, not for a long time, and I would spend it very, very carefully so that I would not have to come bothering you again for years!"

"You do not bother me," Milly replied. "It only worries me what I am to do with you."

"Do you not think it was lucky that this offer came just at the moment when I arrived and asked for your help? And we were, if you remember, talking about the things I could do."

"Acting was not one of them!" Milly snapped.

"That is the whole point," Helga said obstinately. "I will not have to act! The Duke would think I was acting because he would believe me to be an actress, but I would just have to be myself, though of course on my best manners!"

"It is impossible!" Milly said.

But Helga knew she was weakening.

*   *   *

Annie took Helga down to watch from the wings her aunt's sketch in which she played the part of a revengeful and clever young woman.

It was not the same, Helga thought, as seeing it in its proper perspective from the auditorium.

At the same time, the lights, the scenery, and the tall, beautiful Gaiety Girls waiting to go on in the next episode seemed to have stepped out of a Fairyland which she had dreamt about but had never found.

Before her aunt's sketch had completely ended, Annie hurried Helga back to the Dressing Room, so that she missed the clever *dénouement*.

"There's one more turn, then there's the interval," she said, "and I don't know whether your aunt will want you to meet His Grace. I heard him say as 'ow he was coming back."

"I would like to meet him," Helga said.

She was thinking the same thing when Milly, looking flushed and happy after the tremendous applause she had received, came in through the door.

"It went well tonight, Annie," she said.

"That's 'cause you were putting your heart into it," Annie replied. "Different from what happened last week."

Milly did not answer. She knew that Annie was speaking the truth, and because for the moment she had forgotten Christofer she had been able to act with her old expertise which had made her an important member of the cast.

Then as she heard the noise outside of the girls going down for the last *tableau* before the interval, she said to Helga:

"Go back behind the curtain, child, and whatever is

35

said, and whatever happens, you are not to make a sound. Do you understand?"

"Yes, of course," Helga replied. "And you looked lovely, Aunt Millicent, you really did!"

Milly smiled a little complacently. It was something she had heard so often, and for a moment she had forgotten her age and the menacing fear of being unwanted.

The Duke of Rocklington had come to her with his troubles, and that in itself was a compliment which everybody in the Gaiety would appreciate if they knew about it, and would understand.

Then she knew that for her own safety and her own future she had to do what he asked.

She had to believe that there was no alternative and that it was "meant" that Helga should appear at this particular time.

All the same, she was afraid of doing the wrong thing: afraid too for Helga.

The girl was so young, so lovely, and so obviously inexperienced.

Annie was helping her into the gown she would require for the First Act of the next half, and as she did up the last button there was a knock on the door.

Milly looked round to make quite certain that Helga was hidden and the curtain was in place before she said:

"Come in!"

As she expected, the Duke, seeming once again to fill the small room with his presence, appeared.

"You were excellent, Milly, absolutely excellent tonight!"

Annie withdrew and the Duke put his hand on Milly's shoulder to say:

"I know what you have been going through, but Christofer, of all people, would not want you to give in, but to rise above it, and that is what you have done this evening."

The Duke spoke kindly, and Milly felt the tears come into her eyes.

Then because her eyelashes were thick with mascara she brushed them quickly away.

"I thank Your Grace," she said. "You are very kind."

"And now are you going to be kind to me?"

There was a little pause, almost as if Milly were contemplating a deep pool and wondering whether she dare jump into it. Then she said:

"I have an idea I can find someone who would suit your requirements, Your Grace. But, before I do so, I want you to give me your solemn promise."

The Duke looked surprised.

"About what?"

"The girl I have in mind is very young, and very unsophisticated."

"She will hardly remain so for long if she has chosen the stage as her career," the Duke observed cynically.

"That may be true," Milly agreed. "At the same time, I do not wish to be instrumental in the awakening of her to the difficulties and problems that beset all young women in our profession, as Your Grace is well aware."

The Duke nodded and Milly went on:

"If I bring her to you, will you swear on everything you hold Holy that after she has played the part you want, you will return her to me as—unspoiled as she is at the moment?"

Milly had actually wanted to say "untouched" but

37

remembered that Helga was listening and thought it might be too revealing a word.

The Duke laughed lightly.

"My dear Milly, if that is what is troubling you— forget it! I should have thought you knew my taste in women by now. I like them sophisticated, intelligent, and, of course, expert in what the French call *les sciences galantes*. I have no use for young girls."

Milly gave a little sigh.

"If that is true, Your Grace, and if you will give me the assurance I have asked of you, then I will introduce you to the young woman I have in mind, and you can tell her exactly the part you wish her to play."

"I knew you would not fail me, Milly," the Duke said, "and I feel sure too that you can put to good use the one thousand pounds I am willing to pay you for being so helpful."

He rose to his feet and once again he put his hand on her shoulder.

"I understand that Christofer Forsythe could not leave you very much. It must be worrying for you."

"Who told you that?" Milly asked in a voice that tried to be defiant.

"I heard from somebody who knows his wife that she was boasting of how she had her revenge in that Christofer left a load of debts, and nothing else."

Milly closed her eyes for a moment as if to shut out the pain. Then she said:

"I understand now why you are being so kind to me, Your Grace, and I am very grateful."

"On the contrary, you are going to be kind to me,"

the Duke said, "because as I am sure you understand, Milly, there is nobody else I could ask who would understand exactly what I require."

She did not speak and he said:

"I saw your brother the other day at the Club. I suppose whatever the circumstances in which you find yourself, he would not welcome you back into the family fold?"

"Certainly not!" Milly replied. "I am a 'fallen woman' and 'beyond the pale'! I shall never be forgiven for having caused a scandal."

"That is what I thought," the Duke said.

Milly knew that he had deliberately augmented the sum he had been prepared to pay because he knew she was in need and as he was turning away she caught hold of his hand.

"I want to say thank you," she said, "but I am not quite certain how I can find the right words."

"You can thank me tomorrow," the Duke replied. "I will call for you at your flat at a half after twelve and take you, and my prospective 'fiancée' to some quiet place for luncheon. I say 'quiet' because I think it would be a mistake for someone to see us all together."

"A great mistake!" Milly said firmly. "I therefore suggest that Your Grace calls after luncheon and you meet the young woman in question in my flat, where there will be no curious eyes and no one to start tittle-tattle. I have no need to remind you that the Duke of Rocklington is always news."

The Duke laughed.

"That is true, and you are very wise, Milly. I will call on you at about two-thirty, and will you please arrange that the following day your protegée will be ready to leave with me for Rock fairly early? I want to be home before the rest of my party arrives."

"Very well," Milly replied, "and I only hope everything will go off smoothly."

There was a little tremor in her voice because she could not help feeling apprehensive, but the Duke merely said:

"Leave everything to me. I am a very good Stage Manager as long as I have the right actress in the right parts."

He picked up his hat and stick, and as Milly gave him her hand he bent over it, then walked towards the door.

"Thank you, Milly," he said as he reached it. "I will see that you never regret helping me in my hour of need."

Then he was gone and with a little cry Helga came from behind the curtain.

"You agreed! Oh, Aunt Millicent, you agreed! I was so afraid you would change your mind at the last moment!"

Milly sat down on a chair and put her hands up to her head.

"I am not at all happy about it, Helga. I am terrified in case I have done the wrong thing."

"I do not see how it can be wrong," Helga said.

Milly wanted to reply that there were a million ways, but instead she said:

"We will talk about it tonight when we get home, and I only hope you have some decent clothes to wear."

Helga gave a little cry.

"Oh, Aunt Millicent, I had not thought about that until

now! I am afraid they are not very smart and most of them are very old. When Mama was so ill there was no chance for us to go shopping, and as Steppapa did not like me, he grudged me every penny I asked for myself."

This was a snag Milly had not expected. Then she called Annie.

"Tell Nora I want to speak to her."

"I 'spect she's busy," Annie answered.

"She will not be too busy to see me," Milly said firmly. "Tell her it is of great importance."

Annie shrugged her shoulders, but she disappeared to find Nora and Helga asked:

"Who is it that you want to see?"

"The wardrobe mistress," Milly explained. "I do not suppose there will be anything here that will not be spectacular and much too overdressed for a well-behaved young woman who would be likely to marry the Duke of Rocklington—but we can but try our luck."

Helga however was wildly excited when Nora, a worried-looking woman of fifty, came hurrying to the Dressing Room saying:

"I considers it very inconvenient of you, Miss Melrose, to send for me at this moment!"

"It is always inconvenient for you, Nora!" Milly laughed. "But we want your help, and we want it desperately."

Nora looked at Helga curiously.

"Who's this?" she asked. "I've not seen her before!"

"You have not seen her before because she has not been here before," Milly explained, "but she is playing a small part, and I am telling you this in confidence, and

41

you must promise it will go no further."

"I promise! I promise!" Nora said in a rising tone. "What is it?"

"This young lady has been asked to appear in an amateur Play that is to be performed at the Duke of Rocklington's house over the weekend. If anyone gets to hear about it, you will understand that half the cast will be up in arms at not being invited."

"That's true enough!" Nora agreed.

"Now what this role needs," Milly went on quickly, "are some gowns that show she is in mourning, but without being too dreary, if you know what I mean."

"I s'pose what you're sayin' is lilac, purple, grey, and perhaps black net," Nora reeled off.

"Exactly!" Milly agreed.

"Then I think it's unlikely I've got anything of the sort to offer you."

"Please, Nora," Milly begged, "I am sure I am not mistaken that there was a sketch in the last Show where Connie wore a gown of very pale lilac."

Nora thought for a minute, then she said:

"You're right! I wonder where that's bin put?"

"Be an angel and try to find it," Milly begged. "I am sure it was a young girl's dress with not much trimming, and very simple."

"If it's as plain as that, it's very likely bin used for a dish cleaner!" Nora retorted.

She went away and returned very much later, in fact just before the Finale of the whole Show with an armful of clothes.

When she saw them Helga exclaimed with delight, and although they were all made in particularly attractive colours, at the same time there was nothing ostensibly theatrical about them.

"I knew I was right about that sketch!" Milly declared. *"The Unwanted Visitor* it was called."

"That's right!" Nora agreed. "The girl arrives to stay in th' country and feels a reg'lar Cinderella in front of all them rich an' overdressed relations."

Helga wished she could have seen the Play. At the same time it was difficult to think of anything but the beautiful gowns which Nora was helping her into.

She tried them on one after another and although two were a little long, the rest fitted almost perfectly.

"I've a feeling we shall soon have you on our boards," Nora said. "You've got the right figure for it, you're tall enough, an' it's only a question of time before the Guv'nor notices you."

"That is one thing he must not do," Milly said. "I have told you, Nora, that no one is to talk about what is happening, or else His Grace will be very angry. As you are well aware, the other girls would tear him in pieces in order to stay at Rock and act for him."

"My lips're sealed!" Nora promised. "You can trust me. But I still say this young woman'd look very pretty across th' footlights."

"We will think about that another time," Milly said.

Then Helga's gowns were put into a leather case and Joe was told to carry them out to Miss Melrose's carriage.

It surprised Helga to find that her aunt had a very comfortable carriage drawn by two horses with two footmen on the box waiting to take her back from the Theatre.

Only as they drove off, after Milly had been besieged by a lot of autograph hunters did she ask:

"Is this carriage yours, Aunt Millicent?"

"No, dear, it was lent to me by a friend," Milly replied.

Because of the way she spoke, Helga did not ask any more questions.

But Milly was thinking that a thousand pounds would enable her to own her own carriage for a while and not have to be beholden to Sir Emanuel.

At the same time, she thought it would be an extravagance when he was only too willing to lend her one of his.

'There are so many things to be sorted out, when I have the money,' Milly thought.

But she decided to set her own problems on one side while for the moment she concentrated on Helga.

*   *   *

A bed was made up for Helga on the sofa in Milly's Sitting Room and when at last she was alone in the darkness she said a prayer of thankfulness that her aunt had been so kind.

Now she felt at least there was some hope for her in the future.

She had been desperately afraid when she ran away to London that after the years of silence between her mother and her sister, she would be turned away from the stage door.

That would have meant that she would have had to find somewhere else to hide from her stepfather, who, she was quite certain, would be searching for her.

Even if her stepfather did not wish to find her, Bernard

Howell would no doubt consider that chasing her down would be as exciting as a fox hunt.

"I have been lucky, so very, very lucky," Helga told herself as she snuggled down on the rather narrow sofa.

The one thousand pounds would ensure her safety, she reckoned, for at least two years, even if she could find no way of earning any extra money.

It was a gift from God, she decided, a gift that had come at exactly the right moment.

'Mama is watching over me,' she thought to herself, 'and making sure that I am not left at the mercy of Steppapa or his horrible friends.'

Because she was so thankful, she said her prayers for the second time.

Then because it had been such a tiring, if exciting day, she fell asleep.

chapter three

"How do I look, Aunt Millicent?" Helga cried as she came into her aunt's bedroom wearing one of the gowns she had brought from the Gaiety.

It was a very pale lilac and obviously designed to make whoever wore it look very young.

At the same time it gave her a sylphlike, extremely elegant figure with a tiny waist and only a few folds at the back to echo the now departed bustle.

"I think you look lovely, dear," Milly replied.

She was sitting at her dressing table and as she turned round it was almost a blow to see how young and fresh Helga looked compared to her own face which she had been regarding in the mirror.

Her niece did not resemble her, which she thought was a good thing, but she could remember feeling when she was very young, as Helga was, that the whole world

47

was full of sunshine and it was not only outside, but inside her.

That was what she was sure Helga was feeling now as she wore for the first time in her life, a really expensive and beautifully made gown.

"I think this is the prettiest one of them all," Helga said, "so perhaps I had better wear it this afternoon to meet the Duke."

"Yes, that is a good idea," Milly answered, "and I have some flowers of exactly the same colour that I can give you so that you can change the decoration on your hat to match it."

"That is a wonderful idea!" Helga approved. "You are clever, Aunt Millicent!"

Milly turned round from the stool in front of her dressing table so that she had her back to the mirror and was facing Helga.

"Come to sit down, Helga," she said, "I want to talk to you before you set out on this wild adventure. The thought of it has kept me awake all night."

"I was afraid of that," Helga said in a soft voice, "but do not worry. I really can look after myself, and I am sure too that Mama will be looking after me because she is so glad that I came to you as she told me to do."

"I am quite certain your mother would not be pleased at the idea of your coming into contact, in these strange circumstances, with the Duke of Rocklington," Milly said, choosing her words.

"I thought he sounded rather nice," Helga said, "and you told him he was not to spoil me, whatever that might mean."

"I want to tell you about the Duke," Milly said quickly. "He is an extremely attractive man, and very pleasant to meet. But, Helga, what really worries me is that you might fall in love with him."

Helga looked at Milly wide-eyed, then she laughed.

"Oh, Aunt Millicent, I would not think of such a thing!" she said. "I am sure I shall admire him and think him magnificent, but naturally I would not expect him to be at all interested in me. Therefore it would be very stupid if I presumed to love him as a man."

Milly did not speak, and after a moment Helga went on:

"I have thought about falling in love, and I would like to find somebody like Papa who loved Mama so much that he felt miserable if he had to leave her even for a day when he used to go away to buy horses."

"And that is what I hope you will find, dear," Milly said, "but it will not be with the Duke of Rocklington."

"No, of course not!" Helga agreed. "Perhaps one day I will meet somebody quite ordinary, a man I can help and look after, as he will look after me. Then we can get married, live in the country, and have lots of children!"

Milly laughed.

"I see you have it all planned!"

"I tell myself stories of what I want," Helga said, "especially since I became so frightened of Mr. Howell."

She gave a little shiver as she spoke and Milly said:

"You can forget about him. I am sure he will not expect you to be with me and certainly not with the Duke of Rocklington."

"I am sure the Duke would not know anybody so horrible," Helga agreed with a smile, "or Steppapa for that matter!"

Milly thought they had come a long way off the subject she wanted to discuss and she said firmly:

"I have told you not to fall in love with the Duke, Helga, at the same time you are going to his house in a very vulnerable position."

Helga was listening wide-eyed as Milly went on:

"To begin with, you are well aware that no Lady, like for example your mama, would accept a large sum for playing a part which involved a deliberate deception, and no Lady would pretend to be an actress."

To her surprise Helga gave a little laugh.

"The Duke thinks it is the other way around," she said. "He thinks I am an actress pretending to be a Lady."

"Which makes it all the more difficult," Milly said sharply.

"I cannot see why," Helga said.

"It could put you in an embarrassing position," Milly explained, "if the Duke, although I think it is unlikely, behaved in a familiar manner which your mother would not approve."

Now Helga's eyes seemed to fill her whole face and she asked:

"What do you mean by that, Aunt Millicent?"

"I mean," Milly replied slowly, "that he might try to kiss you, which you definitely must not allow, and you must promise me—you must give me your word of honour—that you will lock your door when you go to bed at night."

Helga looked puzzled.

"Lock my door?" she repeated. "But why?"

For a moment Milly contemplated telling her the truth. Then she thought that would be a mistake and said instead:

"Sometimes in large house parties," she said a little lamely, "the Gentlemen have too much to drink at dinner, and if the house is unfamiliar to them they lose their way. In consequence, a man might come into your bedroom after you had gone to sleep and frighten you."

"That sounds a very peculiar way to behave in a Ducal household," Helga said. "Steppapa and his friends used to drink far too much, but when they started to talk in a way which Mama did not approve of, she always left the Dining Room."

"That should not happen at Rock," Milly said. "At the same time, there is always a 'black sheep' in every fold and that is why I am telling you, and I expect you to obey me, Helga, to lock your door."

"But of course I will, Aunt Millicent, if it makes you happy," Helga promised. "I think men when they have had too much to drink and get red in the face and 'swimmy' in the eyes are disgusting!"

"I think so too," Milly said, "and that is why you must be careful not to be involved with anyone like that."

"I certainly will not," Helga promised, "so, please, do not worry. I will be very good and do exactly what you say, and when I come back to London with a thousand pounds to spend, it will be very, very exciting!"

"Very!" Milly agreed.

At the same time she was worried.

It seemed to her impossible that this child, who knew absolutely nothing about life, could cope in any way with a man like the Duke of Rocklington.

After they had eaten a light luncheon in Milly's flat they both waited rather nervously for the Duke to arrive, and if the truth be told, Milly was the more on edge.

Everything Helga said and everything she did took Milly back to her own girlhood and made her remember how strictly she had been brought up and how little she had known of the world outside.

She had almost forgotten in the years that she had been with Christofer and then at the Gaiety how a girl who was born a Lady was isolated from everything that might shock or even surprise her and how completely ignorant she was of men as a sex.

When Christofer swept her off her feet and she ran away with him, she had experienced so much that was astonishing and not in the least what she had expected.

Looking back, she knew how fortunate she had been to find a man who loved her so much that he was very gentle and patient in teaching her al! she had known as a woman.

But could that possibly happen to Helga when she was being pitchforked into the most sophisticated, the most racy circle that existed in the whole of the Social World?

The Prince of Wales was restrained to a certain extent by his beautiful Danish wife, though his love affairs had certainly shocked the Court and were talked about from one end of the country to the other.

But for the Duke of Rocklington there was no such

restraint. Although it had not interested her before, Milly could now look back and count dozens of beautiful women with whom he had associated both in his own world and in that of the Theatre.

"I find beauty attracts me like a magnet!" she had heard him say once at a party.

The unfortunate thing was she thought now, that he drew women in the same way.

"He is magnetic," she told herself, and knew it must be a mistake, a great mistake, for Helga to come in contact with him.

But how could she refuse to help this man who could, if he wished, have her turned away from the Gaiety tomorrow morning, and secondly deprive not only Helga of a large sum of money, but also herself when she so badly needed it.

'I will just have to pray that nothing will go wrong,' she thought.

Helga, feeling the lecture was over, was chattering happily about her gowns and the accessories which would go with them.

Milly lent her a number of things she thought she might require and Helga had promised to be very careful to bring them back undamaged.

There were little satin handbags to carry in the evening, ribbons to wear round her white gowns to accentuate her small waist, which was all the fashion.

Helga looked entrancing in everything she put on. At the same time Milly realised that although they might have come from the Gaiety, the gowns, while looking expensive, were not in the least *outré* or overdressed for a débutante.

Then just before the Duke arrived she gave a little scream of horror.

"What is it?" Helga asked.

"I nearly forgot!" Milly said. "Do you realise we have not yet decided on a name for you? It is quite impossible for you to be a Wensley, in case the Duke knows of your father."

"Of course, I understand," Helga said, "and it was very stupid of me to forget that."

"I think it would be a good idea," Milly said, thinking it over, "that you should have a rather grand, pretentious English name which we can say you are going to use on the stage but which will also seem quite suitable for a Duke's *fiancée*."

"You are right, Aunt Millicent," Helga agreed. "What name shall we choose?"

"Now, let me think . . ." Milly said. "The Duke has a house in London in Grosvenor Square, and there are quite a number of people called Grosvenor."

"Helga Grosvenor! That sounds very exciting!"

"I suppose really we should change your Christian name too," Milly said reflectively.

Helga gave a little cry.

"Oh, no, please do not do that, Aunt Millicent! I shall never remember to answer to another one, and Mama chose it especially when I was born, because she had some Norwegian blood in her and she thought it would give me Viking power, which is what I feel I have when I tell fortunes."

"I am rather suspicious of this fortune-telling," Milly said. "I should not mention it to the Duke if I were you. He might think you are a Gypsy, or something."

Helga laughed.

"I do not look very like one."

That was certainly true, for with her very fair hair, her eyes which flecked with gold seemed to have caught the sunshine, and her complexion, which was as clear as any Gainsborough beauty, Helga certainly had nothing in common with the dark-skinned, black-haired Gypsies.

Milly was remembering how they used to camp on her father's estate at home when they were children.

"Well, all I can hope," she said somewhat tartly, "is that your 'Viking power' does not get you into trouble. If you predict anything that people do not like, or turns out to be unlucky, you will certainly make a bitter enemy!"

At two-thirty precisely the Duke arrived.

When he came into Milly's Sitting Room, which was not very large, Helga felt he filled the whole room, not only because he was so tall, but also because his personality seemed to vibrate from him.

It was what she had expected from hearing his voice, though unable to see him.

What she had not realised was that any man could be so handsome.

First he greeted Milly, then as he turned to look at her Helga felt as if his eyes not only took in her outward appearance but penetrated deep inside her.

It was as if he searched for something that was not immediately apparent.

It was just an impression she had.

Then he smiled in what she thought was an irresistible manner as Milly said:

"May I introduce Miss Helga Grosvenor? She says

she will be glad to help you, by playing the part you require."

The Duke took Helga's hand in his and she felt the strength of his fingers and again the vibrations that were so very obvious when he had come into the room.

"I am extremely grateful to you, Miss Grosvenor," he said. "Shall we sit down and have a talk about it, and I will tell you exactly what I want you to do?"

"I only hope I shall not make any mistakes."

"As you will be constantly with me, that will be impossible," the Duke said.

He seated himself in an armchair and Milly sat in another, leaving Helga to sit on the small sofa which faced the mantelpiece.

"I imagine Miss Melrose has already told you," the Duke began, "the reason why I require somebody to act the part of my *fiancée* at my house party which is to take place at Rock this weekend."

"Yes, Miss Melrose explained that you have an American guest who wishes you to marry his daughter," Helga replied.

"That is correct," the Duke agreed, "and you will understand that as I have no wish to marry anyone, nor do I intend to be married for a very long time, I do not want to be pressured into taking an American bride, with the alternative of causing a great deal of ill will by refusing."

"I do see it is a very difficult position for you," Helga said. "But will your other guests not think it strange that you have suddenly become engaged without their having any knowledge of it?"

The Duke smiled.

"I see you are very quick-brained, Miss Grosvenor," he said, "and I have already thought of that."

He paused for a moment before he said:

"I intend to inform Mr. Vanderfeld, who is my American guest, that I am telling him of my engagement in the strictest secrecy, and entrusting him on his honour not to mention it to anybody."

The Duke looked at Helga as he spoke as if he expected her to ask if Mr. Vanderfeld would not think that strange, but when she did not do so, he said:

"I shall explain to him that the reason for such secrecy is that you are in mourning, and your relatives would be extremely shocked if there was any talk of an engagement until that period was over."

The Duke paused for a moment before he asked:

"Shall we say that you are mourning your father or mother?"

"My . . . mother . . ." Helga said quietly.

She could not help her voice giving a little tremor as she spoke.

"As it happens," Milly interrupted quickly, "Helga has only recently lost her mother."

"I am sorry," the Duke said. "I fear you must miss her."

"Terribly!" Helga said simply.

"Then that is our story," the Duke said in a different tone, "and I think the minute Mr. Vanderfeld realises there is no possible chance of my marrying his daughter, we will be able to get on with our business negotiations, which are very important."

"Are you having a big house party?" Milly asked.

"No, only some of my very special friends," the Duke

replied, "who I know will be nice to Vanderfeld, and with whom he will be impressed."

There was a little twist to his lips as he spoke, and Helga wondered if the American would behave in exactly the way the Duke was expecting, or whether there would be any surprises for him.

She was too shy to say this aloud, and after the Duke had talked to Milly about the Theatre he rose to his feet saying:

"I will collect you at ten o'clock tomorrow morning, Miss Grosvenor, if that is not too early?"

Then before Helga could reply he said:

"No, it is wrong for me to call you 'Miss Grosvenor,' and I like the name Helga, although I have never heard of it before."

"It is Norwegian," Helga explained.

The Duke raised his eyebrows as if he were surprised that an actress should know such a thing, but he merely said:

"It is a charming name, which suits you, and Grosvenor is, as I expect Milly is aware, a very appropriate name for my *fiancée*."

"I have just thought of something," Helga said. "Suppose the other people in the house party ask me about my relatives?"

"You will have to be very evasive," the Duke replied, "and tell them you have been living very quietly in the country and have had no contact with the Grosvenors who live in London."

Because he thought Helga still looked a little worried, he said:

"Leave it to me, I will gloss over all the difficulties,

and I promise you things will not be half as frightening as you are anticipating."

"How do you know that is how I feel?" Helga asked ingenuously.

"Shall I say your eyes are very expressive?" the Duke replied.

He spoke in a dry voice which did not make it sound like a compliment.

Then he left, leaving behind him, Helga thought, as Milly followed him to the door of the flat, a kind of disturbance on the air.

It was as if a miniature typhoon, or perhaps a meteor was a better description, had passed through the Sitting Room.

In the tiny hall where there was room only for a small chair and a minute table the Duke said:

"She is perfect, Milly! I cannot be too grateful to you! I knew if anybody could help me it would be you."

"I only hope nothing will go wrong," Milly said in a worried voice.

"Why should it?" the Duke asked. "I will return Helga to you sometime on Monday."

Milly looked up at him questioningly and he said:

"I have given you my word that I will not do anything to spoil anyone so attractive, and so exactly right for the part I wish her to play."

"Thank you," Milly said.

The Duke drew an envelope from his inside pocket.

"Here is my cheque," he said. "I made it out for two thousand pounds. I did not know your *protegée*'s name then, but I think I can trust you with her share."

He spoke teasingly, and Milly said:

"It is a lot of money, and we are both very grateful."

"As I am to you."

Then he was gone, and Milly went back into the Sitting Room.

"Two thousand pounds, Helga!" she said. "I am going to put yours in your own name into my Bank. I will open an account for you and at least it cannot be stolen."

"I think I am dreaming," Helga said. "When I came to see you yesterday I had only a few pounds left. Now I am a millionairess!"

Milly laughed.

"Not quite! Remember, money does not last for ever!"

"Oh, Aunt Millicent, I can never thank you enough for being so kind to me!"

She put her arms around her aunt's neck and kissed her, but Milly wondered if that was what it would turn out that she had been.

* * *

The Duke's horses were superb and so was the open Cabriolet in which he arrived to drive Helga down to Rock.

To her surprise, an hour earlier his servants had called for her luggage, saying it was to be taken there in a Brake.

"It sounds very grand!" Helga said to Milly.

"You cannot expect the Duke of Rocklington," she replied, "to concern himself with anything so mundane as a trunk! Or even a small parcel, if it can be carried by anybody else!"

They both laughed, and when Helga sat beside the

Duke on the comfortable padded seat and the groom who was to sit rather uncomfortably behind had covered her legs with a fur rug, she felt she was stepping into a dream and none of this could be true.

The Duke's horses moved extremely swiftly and were certainly as magnificent as their master as they swept through the traffic.

Then as the houses were fading into the distance and they were out in the country Helga asked:

"How far is your house from London?"

"Only a little over twenty miles," the Duke replied, "and I so much prefer to drive there than travel by train."

"Of course," Helga agreed, "I have not been in many trains, but when I came to London in one yesterday I thought it was noisy and smelly, and I could not understand anybody wanting to give up horses for the iron wheels of a railway."

The Duke laughed.

"I am afraid these wheels have come to stay, and the next thing I shall have to buy is a motor car."

"Oh, I hope not!" Helga said. "I have been told they are always breaking down."

"I expect somebody will find a cure for that," the Duke said. "In the meantime, I enjoy my horses and I am glad you do too."

"I have never seen such fine animals."

"Have you, as I hope, brought a riding-habit with you?" the Duke asked.

"I have," Helga replied, "even though I was afraid there would be no chance of riding."

She paused, then she said:

"I must be honest and tell you it is not very smart! In

61

fact, it is very old and rather threadbare, and if I wore it, it would be a mistake for Mr. Vanderfeld to see it. It might make him suspicious."

The Duke laughed again.

"Then we must certainly prevent that! So we will go riding either first thing in the morning before he is awake, or when I am quite certain he is engaged in doing something on another part of the estate."

Helga gave a little sigh of relief.

She had brought her riding-habit with her to London but had been afraid when she packed it in the smart trunk her aunt had lent her, that it might be a mistake for the Duke to see any of the clothes that she really owned.

But because she was going to the country she could not help feeling she might have a chance of riding, and it would be something she could not bear to miss.

The only consolation she had had for living in her stepfather's house, which she hated, was that he could afford good horses and allowed her to ride them.

She was quite certain the Duke would have better horses than anybody else.

As if he guessed that was what she was thinking, he said:

"I am presuming that you are a good rider, and I have one or two horses which I think you will enjoy riding, but which I would not as a rule offer to my other lady guests."

"Why not?"

"Because, quite frankly, they do not ride well enough," the Duke said.

"And you think I will?"

"I am working it out logically. You say that your habit is old and threadbare. That means you have worn it a great deal. I also suspect, because you are going on the stage to earn money, that you are not well off. That means you have had to make the best of poor horses and, undoubtedly, as you enjoy riding, you are in consequence a good rider."

Helga gave a little chuckle of delight and clapped her hands together.

"That is very clever of you, and actually it is true!"

"I thought it would be!" the Duke said complacently.

"Do you always work things out in that intricate manner?" Helga asked.

"I find people interesting," the Duke replied, "and quite frankly, Helga, I am very intrigued about you."

"Why is that?"

"Because first of all it seems extraordinary that, looking as you do, I have not seen or heard about you before, which I should undoubtedly have done if you had been on the stage in London. And secondly that Milly should have magicked you up out of nowhere at such short notice."

He paused before he asked:

"Are you an illusion? Will you perhaps suddenly disappear so that I shall find I am driving alone?"

"I hope not—at least not until I have seen Rock!" Helga said quickly.

"You have heard of it before?"

Helga hesitated a moment, then told him the truth.

"A long time ago," she said, "I saw sketches of it in *The Illustrated London News* and an article written about

63

you. I did not think of it until last night. Then I remembered reading it and thinking how interesting it all was."

"I remember that article," the Duke said. "It must have been three or four years ago. You could not have been very old."

"Fifteen," Helga said. "My mother often talked to me of big houses, and I am therefore very interested in them."

"Why should she have done that?"

It struck Helga that perhaps she had been indiscreet, and she said after a moment's pause:

"Perhaps because we lived in such a very small house. It was a little old Manor and yet although we were very poor we were very happy."

"And your mother envied those who were rich and lived in big houses?" the Duke asked, almost as if he wanted to find fault.

"I do not think that 'envy' is the right word," Helga protested, "but she was interested, and made me learn about architecture and of course the contents of houses such as yours. Have you some very fine pictures?"

"I think that is a good description of them," the Duke said.

"Then please will you make sure I have time to look at every one of them."

The Duke turned his head to look at her swiftly, but she was staring ahead and she did not see the quizzical look in his eyes.

He was actually thinking he could not remember ever having met an actress who had been interested in pictures or indeed in anything else which did not concern the stage or what some man could provide for her.

Quite a number of ambitious women had sought to

ingratiate themselves with him by talking about his possessions.

It had always been very obvious what their motive was in doing so, but the way in which Helga spoke was different.

She was not begging him personally to show her his pictures; she just wanted to see them for herself.

He found himself wondering what she actually felt about coming to Rock and acting the part he required of her, apart from the fact that she was making a great deal of money out of it.

"Why did you decide to go on the stage?" he asked. "And where have you appeared so far?"

He was expecting the answer to be that it was in the Provinces, but Helga had already thought this out carefully and she replied:

"I have not actually acted anywhere yet, I am merely preparing to do so by taking lessons."

"What sort of lessons?"

"Singing, elocution, and of course dancing."

As she spoke she hoped the Duke would not ask her where these lessons took place and decided if he did she would say it had been in the country.

"I should not have thought you required such tuition where elocution is concerned, Helga. You speak very well, and you have an exceedingly large vocabulary for..."

He decided the end he had intended would have sounded rude and substituted:

"... for somebody of your age."

"Thank you," Helga said. "My mother used to make me read aloud to her when I was very little, and was very insistent that I pronounced my words correctly."

She thought as she spoke that the Duke could hardly find that kind of answer suspicious.

She was unaware that in fact he was thinking that the mothers of most actresses would not have known if a word was correctly pronounced or not.

"Have you known Milly for long?" he enquired.

This was fortunately a question that Milly had foreseen, and she had said to Helga:

"If the Duke asks you that, say that I am an old friend of your father's. Not your mother's. Remember that as a member of the Gaiety Theatre I have known many more men than women."

"Why is that?" Helga had asked innocently.

"Because as a rule women do not approve of actresses and Ladies are not allowed to speak to them."

"I think that is because they are jealous!" Helga said loyally. "Or they are just stuffy and disagreeable about people who go on the stage—like Uncle Richard?"

"You must not forget I shocked my father and mother when I ran away from home," Milly said, "and I have never seen your mother all these years."

"I think Mama used to long to see you," Helga said, "but we were too poor to come to London. I think too, although she never said so, she was afraid because you were so glamorous and gay that you would find us very dull and unexciting."

Milly made a choking sound that was almost a sob.

"I wish I had known about that," she said. "I just believed that everybody, including your mother, was looking down their noses and condemning me."

"Mama would never have done that, and I know she

loved you," Helga said, "or she would not have sent me to you when she was dying."

The thought of her mother made Helga feel like crying, but she knew it was something she must not do.

Then as they drove on the Duke asked:

"What is the matter? You looked so happy when we started off from London, and now suddenly everything has changed and I feel there is a cloud in your sky. What is it?"

Helga turned her face to look at him in astonishment.

"How can you talk like that? How can you be so perceptive?"

"Shall I say it is somewhat unusual for me to feel as I do about you," the Duke replied, "but you are as transparent as a mountain stream and I can almost read your thoughts."

"That is something you must not do," Helga said quickly.

"Why not? Are they so secret?"

"Yes, they are!"

"Then if they worry you, I suggest it would be a good thing to share your problems, whatever they are, with someone else."

"I have not said I have any problems," Helga said defiantly.

"Now I am using my perception," the Duke said, "and I am quite certain you have a problem. I am not sure what it is, but it is something that has frightened you."

He paused before he went on:

"When I came into Milly's Sitting Room yesterday I thought you were frightened of me. But now I have the most convincing feeling that it is something much deeper than that: something which has nothing to do with being frightened of me, but which has nevertheless made you afraid."

Helga drew in her breath.

"Now you are being clairvoyant," she said, "and that is something I am myself when I am telling fortunes."

"You tell fortunes?" the Duke asked.

Too late Helga remembered Milly had told her she was not to mention this.

"Occasionally," she said evasively.

"And they come true?"

"Sometimes."

"This is interesting," the Duke said. "I am being perceptive about you, but you can be perceptive about other people. I have always suspected that in fortune-telling there is a great deal of thought-reading."

"Only superficially," Helga said. "Then one sees, beyond what they are thinking, the things that will happen in the future, and that is something far deeper and more fundamental than thought."

She spoke positively because the subject interested her.

Then once again she thought she had made a mistake as the Duke said:

"I find this extraordinarily intriguing, but for the moment I want to get back to the reason why you are afraid, and who has frightened you."

"That is something I must not tell you."

"But you admit it is true?"

"I am trying to admit nothing," she said, "but you are making it very difficult for me."

The Duke gave a little laugh, and they drove on.

68

Because the horses were moving so swiftly, it was impossible to talk, for which Helga was thankful.

She had the uncomfortable feeling she had made a mistake and her Aunt Millicent would not have been pleased with her.

At the same time she found it, in her turn, extremely intriguing that he should be perceptive about her, and also be interested in her perceptions about other people.

Then they were passing through a small village with well-tended cottages, their gardens ablaze with flowers, and a few seconds later they turned in at some huge ornamental wrought-iron gates with a lodge on either side of them.

Helga drew in her breath.

There was a drive ahead with oak trees on either side of it. Then at the far end she saw a house that might have stepped straight out of her dreams.

It was in fact, very like the sketch she had seen of it so many years ago: enormous, overwhelming, and at the same time very beautiful.

So beautiful that for a moment she was not frightened, but only carried away by feeling it was everything a Ducal home should be, and a fitting background for the Duke.

"Now I can show you Rock!" he said quietly. "I shall be very interested to hear what you think about it."

"It is . . . even more lovely than I expected," Helga said, "and now I am definitely afraid I might . . . wake up!"

The Duke was laughing as he drove on.

chapter four

COMING down the huge staircase, the Rocklington ancestors in gold frames on the walls and the flags which
they had won in battle arranged around the marble fireplace, Helga felt that now, definitely, she had stepped
into her dream and was a part of it.

The gown she was wearing was a very simple girl's
dress in white trimmed with lace, and that too made her
feel like a Fairy Princess, so that her eyes were bright
as stars.

Her feet seemed almost to fly down the stairs until
she reached the hall.

The Duke had told her she was to meet Mr. Vanderfeld
before dinner, as he and his daughter were arriving late
and would only just have time to change.

This meant they would not yet have met any of the

rest of the house party to whom Helga had been introduced earlier in the evening.

After their arrival at Rock, the Duke had shown her the stables before luncheon, and when the meal, at which they were alone, was over, he had taken her around his garden, his hothouses, and she had been entranced by everything she saw.

She was intelligent enough to realise that the reason that he had asked her to come to Rock far earlier than the other guests was to make sure she played her part perfectly and did nothing that would betray her as being an actress rather than a Lady.

She noticed that he was watching what cutlery she chose and the way she held her glass at luncheon.

She thought with a smile that her mother would feel insulted that he should be critical.

At the same time she kept reminding herself that she was an actress and the Duke thought she was giving a performance, and she must be careful for her aunt's sake not to betray her real identity.

It was also a great satisfaction to know she had escaped from her stepfather and Bernard Howell.

Never would it cross their minds to look for her at Rock.

"I am safe! I am safe!" she told herself when she was alone in the beautiful bedroom which was far grander than any room she had ever slept in before.

But there was still a lurking fear that things could not be so perfect as they seemed and she might in fact have a rude awakening.

Now all she was aware of was that in the crucial first moment when she met Mr. Vanderfeld, if she did anything wrong, it might arouse his suspicions.

The rest of the party were to meet in the Silver Salon before dinner, but Helga had been told to come to the Duke's Private Study which was farther down a corridor, filled with treasures at which she longed to stop and look.

She had her instructions, and as a footman opened the door for her she saw the Duke was standing in front of the mantelpiece and beside him stood a middle-aged man who was obviously Cyrus Vanderfeld.

The two men were in deep conversation and when she entered, the Duke looked up and said with a smile:

"Ah, here you are, Helga!"

Then as she walked towards him he said to Mr. Vanderfeld:

"I asked you to meet me here in this room, before we joined the rest of my party, for a very special reason."

"What can that be?" Mr. Vanderfeld asked with a pronounced American accent.

"I thought it only right," the Duke said, "since, as you suggested, I would be joining you in America later in the year, that I should let you into a secret."

Mr. Vanderfeld did not speak.

He was looking at Helga, obviously waiting to be introduced.

"It is a secret," the Duke continued, "of which only you and no one else will be aware, but as we are already closely connected in business I want you to be the first person to meet my future wife—Miss Helga Grosvenor!"

The Duke spoke quietly and almost soothingly, and Helga was aware that as he had made the introduction, Mr. Vanderfeld started and there was a frown between his thick eyebrows.

"Your future wife, Duke?" he exclaimed. "Well, this is a surprise!"

Helga held out her hand.

"I have heard a great deal about you, Mr. Vanderfeld," she said, "and how very, very clever you are."

Mr. Vanderfeld took her hand.

At the same time he said to the Duke:

"You're sure full of surprises! I had no idea you were thinking of getting married. I had always heard you were an avowed bachelor."

"That was true," the Duke replied, "but now you have seen Miss Grosvenor, I think you will understand why I have changed my mind."

"Sure, sure!" Mr. Vanderfeld said as if he were aware this was a compliment he should have made himself.

"You must let me fill up your glass," the Duke said genially, "so that you can wish us health and happiness. At the same time, Helga and I trust you not to breathe a word of this to anybody else in the party."

"You can trust me, Duke," Mr. Vanderfeld said heartily, "but why does there have to be any secrecy about your engagement?"

"Sadly, my *fiancée* is in mourning for her mother," the Duke explained. "In England it would be considered extremely heartless for her to marry or announce her engagement before the twelve-month period of mourning is over."

"Twelve months!" Mr. Vanderfeld exclaimed. "That's not a custom we have back in America."

"It is different here," the Duke said, "and was, may I say, endorsed by the Queen herself."

"Of course, of course, I remember," Mr. Vanderfeld

said. "Her Majesty mourned Prince Albert for many years."

"So you will understand how shocked the Court would be if it was known that Helga and I had become engaged."

"You can trust me to tell no one!" Mr. Vanderfeld said.

Helga thought that his initial disappointment at the news had passed, and he now accepted the compliment of being the first "in the know."

He certainly sounded sincere as he raised his glass to say:

"May I wish you both many years of happiness together? And of course a large number of heirs to succeed to this fine house!"

Helga looked shy and the Duke said hastily:

"Now you are embarrassing my *fiancée*, and I think we should join the others in the Silver Salon, where your daughter will be waiting for you."

Mr. Vanderfeld opened his lips as if he were about to say that his daughter would be very disappointed when she knew there was no longer any chance of her being a Duchess.

Then he remembered his promise and said:

"I'm sure Miss Grosvenor and Virginia will get along fine."

"I hope they will," the Duke agreed, "and Helga is particularly interested in the Ranch you own in Texas, where I believe your horses are outstanding!"

"I look forward to showing them to you, Duke," Mr. Vanderfeld replied.

When they joined the rest of the party, who were drinking champagne in the Silver Salon, Helga thought it would be impossible to see a collection of so many beautiful women so elegantly dressed anywhere else except perhaps on stage at the Gaiety.

The gentlemen too looked very impressive in their evening clothes, and she could understand that Virginia Vanderfeld was looking around her with an awed expression in her eyes.

A very pretty girl, with the pronounced American chin, her hair swept back in a style that had just been made fashionable by Charles Dana Gibson.

It looked far more attractive, Helga thought, than the teapot-handle knot which most women wore on top of their heads.

She decided it was a fashion she could copy quite easily without feeling she looked out of place.

She thought however that quite a number of the Ladies, wearing tiaras and glittering with jewels, were looking at her in surprise as if they could not imagine why she had been included in the party.

Then because perceptively she could read their thoughts, she knew they solved the problem by deciding that the Duke had asked her because Miss Vanderfeld was also young.

Dinner in the huge Baronial Dining Hall with the gold candelabra on the table decorated with orchids was a delight in itself.

Helga chatted away quite happily with the gentlemen on either side of her.

Only one of them seemed a little curious as to who she was and why he had not met her before, but she managed to parry his questions quite adroitly.

Only as the Ladies withdrew into the Drawing Room

did she find herself interrogated in a far more subtle and penetrating manner.

The Countess of Carrington, who appeared to be acting as hostess to the Duke, was the most beautiful woman Helga had ever seen with the exception of her Aunt Millicent.

She was tall with dark hair and slanting eyes that made everything she said seem to have a double meaning, which made the gentlemen all laugh.

Her gown, which clung to her figure like a snake's skin, was embroidered all over with sequins, and around her neck was a necklace of rubies that matched the tiara on her head.

"You are looking radiant tonight, Betty!" Helga heard one of the other ladies say to her as they moved into the Salon after dinner.

"Why not?" the Countess replied. "You know that Hugo, like the Prince of Wales, expects his women to be spectacular."

"That is certainly something you are."

"How could I be anything else at Rock?" the Countess enquired. "It is always a joy to be hostess here and realise that dear Hugo relies on me to keep everything moving smoothly."

She spoke almost as if she were purring like a cat over a dish of cream.

Helga thought it strange that the Duke should have as a hostess someone who was apparently not a relative.

She suddenly felt nervous when the Countess moved from across the room to where she was sitting on the sofa and sat down beside her.

"Now, you must tell me all about yourself, Miss Grosvenor," she said. "You are the only member of the party I have not met before, and in fact I had no idea that the Duke, who is a very, very dear friend of mine, knew you."

"It was very exciting for me to be asked to Rock," Helga replied. "I have heard about it, of course, and I cannot imagine there is a house in England which is more lovely."

"You are quite right there," the Countess said. "And where you do come from?"

"I have been living in the country," Helga said truthfully.

"Whereabouts?"

"In Gloucestershire."

The Countess wrinkled her smooth lily-white forehead.

"Now let me think—who do I know in Gloucestershire? I have friends everywhere."

"It is quite a big county," Helga said, "and I lived very quietly with my mother, who was in ill health and died recently."

"So you are in mourning?" the Countess questioned.

Helga nodded.

"I hope then that you will not find the festivities that take place this weekend too much for you. If they are, I shall understand if you slip away alone."

"Thank you," Helga said, "but I find everything very interesting, and I am sure my mother, if she were alive, would want me to enjoy myself."

She was well aware as she spoke that the Countess did not like her and was in fact somewhat suspicious.

Helga concentrated on the beautiful woman beside her and told herself she was not really a kind person or interested in anybody's feelings except her own.

It was a relief when another lady came up to speak to the Countess, which diverted her interest into another channel.

As she moved away, Helga had a definite impression that she was hostile and she told herself she must be careful.

When the Gentlemen rejoined them, some of the guests sat down at the Bridge tables and there was also Roulette for those who wished to gamble.

The Duke however decided to show Mr. Vanderfeld and his daughter some of his pictures and he told Helga she could come with them.

It was what she was longing to do, but she knew as they left the Drawing Room that the Countess looked up from the gambling table with an angry expression in her slanting eyes.

The pictures were even more entrancing than Helga had imagined they would be, but after a while Mr. Vanderfeld obviously grew bored. When they reached the Library, with its thousands of books reaching towards the ceiling, at the Duke's suggestion they stopped for a drink.

They sat down in the red leather chairs and sofas which were grouped around the fireplace.

Helga had already found that Virginia Vanderfeld was rather difficult to talk to, and now the two girls lapsed into silence as Mr. Vanderfeld and the Duke began to talk business.

"There's a man I am going to recommend to you, Duke, who I think will manage your business excellently over here," Mr. Vanderfeld said, "and he's cute enough to understand all the 'Ins and Outs' of what we have been discussing as well as I do myself."

"I shall be interested to meet him," the Duke replied. "What is his name?"

"Potter—Cyril Potter," Mr. Vanderfeld answered. "Although I met him only recently, he appears to be a very shrewd operator, and just what you need to get the whole business under way and save yourself a great deal of trouble into the bargain!"

"That certainly appears satisfactory," the Duke said.

Helga had been listening and now, as clearly as if someone were telling her so, she was aware that the man Potter of whom Mr. Vanderfeld was speaking was a crook.

The impression was so strong in her mind that she knew she was not mistaken, for that her clairvoyant "eye" could see him quite clearly and if the Duke accepted him on Mr. Vanderfeld's recommendation, it would be disastrous.

For a moment she felt she must speak out. Then she knew that Mr. Vanderfeld would not believe her and it might antagonise him, which would certainly annoy the Duke.

Helga waited until they began to make their way back into the Salon, with Mr. Vanderfeld still speaking of what an excellent man Potter was and what a help he would be in setting up an office in England.

Then, just before they reached the Salon door, Helga put her hand on the Duke's arm and said:

"May I speak to you for a moment?"

He looked down at her in surprise, almost as if he had forgotten her existence, and said:

"Of course."

Mr. Vanderfeld was stepping ahead of them and he said:

"Go on without me, will you, Vanderfeld. I am sure they will find you a place at the Roulette table."

"I don't really care much for gambling," Mr. Vanderfeld replied, "but I'll sure enjoy watching!"

He walked to the Salon followed by his daughter, and the Duke turned two paces back to say to Helga impatiently:

"Now what is it? Is anything wrong?"

"It is just that . . . I know," she said almost in a whisper, "that this man of whom Mr. Vanderfeld was speaking is not what he . . . appears to be. He is crooked, I am sure of it, and it would be very inadvisable for you to let him handle your business."

She spoke quickly in a nervous little voice, and realised as she expected that the Duke was staring at her incredulously.

"Is this a joke? Do you know this man?" he asked. "What makes you think that what you have just said is true?"

"We talked of my . . . perception on the way here," Helga said, "and I told you that I can tell fortunes. I am absolutely convinced that, although this man Potter may have deceived Mr. Vanderfeld, if you make confidential enquiries about him you will find he is completely dishonest and unreliable and would certainly lose you a great deal of money."

There was silence until the Duke said:

"I can hardly believe that what you are saying is true! However I will make every possible investigation about him before I trust him."

"I beg of you not to trust him," Helga said. "I am never mistaken when I feel about someone as I do now."

"I do not quite understand," the Duke said, "how you can feel so strongly about someone you have not seen and who is not present?"

"That was not necessary because he was so very real to Mr. Vanderfeld," Helga replied. "My perception reaches beyond time and space and, although I cannot explain it, it can be very convincing, as it is at this moment."

"You are certainly full of surprises!" the Duke retorted. "And talking of something quite different, I would like to congratulate you on a brilliant performance so far. When this is over, we must certainly discuss your future, and I cannot help feeling that some of our most distinguished actors and actresses will have to 'look to their laurels'!"

"Now you are teasing me," Helga said, "but I am glad I have not done anything wrong."

"Everything you have done has been perfect!" the Duke said. "I can only say that Milly is a genius for having found you, as I will certainly tell her the moment I return to London."

Then as if he thought it was a mistake to stay away from the party, he walked towards the door of the Salon, standing back to allow Helga to enter first.

As she did so the Countess of Carrington came sweeping towards them, her rubies gleaming like a demon's eyes around her neck and in her hair.

"Where have you been, Hugo?" she demanded. "And

what has Miss Grosvenor been talking to you about in that surreptitious manner, which has kept you standing outside in the hall?"

"I will tell you about it another time," the Duke said casually. "Now I would like to play a game of Bridge."

He walked towards the Bridge table as he spoke and the Countess hung back to say to Helga in a furious tone:

"I suggest, Miss Grosvenor, you do not make a nuisance of yourself by trying to monopolise the Duke's attention when he has so many friends to attend to."

The Countess's eyes flashed as she spoke and Helga, feeling abashed and shy, could only murmur:

"I . . . I am sorry . . . I did not mean to upset . . . anyone."

"Well, you have upset me!" the Countess said.

Then she flounced away, following the Duke to the Bridge table.

Helga left alone looked around and saw Virginia Vanderfeld was also alone and moving to the other end of the room, where there was nothing but a number of empty chairs.

Thinking it was the polite thing to do, she joined her and the American girl said:

"This sure is a fine house, but I don't feel the people in it are very friendly—not like they are back home."

Helga laughed.

"The English have a reputation for being reserved," she said, "but I would like to come to America, especially to see your Ranch."

They sat down side by side on the sofa, and after they had talked about horses Virginia said:

"I wanted to come to Europe with Pa, but what I

minded was leaving my horses behind. I have several entered for the races, but there's little point in it if I am not there to see them run."

She sounded so sad about it that Helga said:

"If you trained them yourself I am sure nothing could be more exciting than seeing them first past the winning post."

"You understand," Virginia said, "but Pa kept saying there would be other years and other races. But I want to be there now!"

"I can understand that."

There was a little pause, then Virginia said:

"It's not only the horses—I have a friend—someone I want to marry, but Pa is determined I shall marry an Englishman and be very, very important."

Because Helga thought it might make it easier for the Duke she said:

"Shall I tell your fortune and see first if your horses will win their races, and then if you will marry the man you want to?"

Virginia's eyes lit up.

"Can you do that?"

Helga looked around the room.

There was a small table with two chairs on the other side of it and she said aloud:

"If we could get hold of a pack of cards they would think we were playing piquet or something, while actually I will be seeing your future."

Virginia jumped to her feet.

Quite unabashed, she went up to one of the Bridge tables that was not being used.

She picked up a pack of cards and came back to Helga.

"Here you are," she said.

"You do not think they will miss them?" Helga asked.

"If they do, they can get some others," Virginia replied. "I always take what I want and leave people to ask questions afterwards."

Helga laughed.

"That is obviously very sensible."

They sat down at the table and on Helga's instructions Virginia shuffled the cards, and Helga picked out the ones that were important and turned them over, one by one.

It was not exactly that the cards themselves were significant, but they enabled her to concentrate on what Virginia was thinking and what lay behind what she was feeling, a method which she had always found helpful.

Then she said after a moment:

"You have one horse whose name begins with a 'Y.'"

"Yacko!" Virginia murmured.

"Well, Yacko will win two races, and when you hear about it you will be very pleased and very happy."

"That's marvellous!" Virginia cried. "I felt he would win, but there is some pretty tough competition where we live."

"I can see your young man quite clearly," Helga went on.

Now she put the cards down and merely looked at Virginia.

"He is very handsome."

"How do you know?" Virginia enquired.

"He has a nice, happy personality, and I am sure—

yes, I am quite sure—that when you go back to America your father will allow you to marry him, and you will be very happy."

"Thank you, thank you!" Virginia said. "That is exactly what I wanted to hear. I've been so miserable all the time I have been in Europe in case he forgets about me while I am away."

"You need not worry about that, and you will make a very beautiful bride and have a very big wedding."

"That's what I want," Virginia said, "and it's only Pa who has these nonsensical ideas about my marrying an Englishman and having a grand title. I don't want a title. I just want to be married to Steve and ride with him on his Ranch which is big, if not bigger than Pa's."

"I am sure you will have all that," Helga said.

As she spoke she felt somebody come up and stand beside her, and looking up she saw it was the Duke.

"Now, what are you two up to?" he enquired.

"Miss Grosvenor's been telling me my fortune," Virginia said, "and it is everything I wanted to hear. I am going to marry the man I love and my horse is going to win two races!"

Feeling embarrassed because the Duke was standing there with an expression on his face she did not understand, Helga hurriedly stacked the cards together.

Then as Virginia jumped up to run across the room to her father and they were alone, the Duke said:

"Have you told her what you believe to be the truth or were you really just 'sweetening the pill' that her father's ambitions are not likely to materialise?"

"I would not think of telling anything but the truth!" Helga said quickly.

"Tomorrow I think I shall ask you to tell my fortune."

Helga looked away from him down at the cards she was holding in her hand.

"I think that might be a mistake and also very difficult," she said.

"Why should you say that?" he enquired.

"Because," she replied, "if I tell you what it will please you to hear, you will suspect that I am only trying to put you in a good temper, while if I tell you something that annoys you it will be very unpleasant for me."

The Duke laughed.

"I think that is a very ingenious way of getting out of a difficult situation! Quite frankly, Helga, I am suspicious of your clairvoyance, which I think you turn on and off like a tap to suit yourself."

"That is not true!" Helga flashed. "You will find when you investigate Mr. Potter what I told you is true."

"I am more interested at the moment in investigating you," the Duke said. "I wonder if I shall succeed in discovering whether you are true or false, straight or crooked, ingenious or very, very skilful as an actress."

As he spoke his eyes were on Helga's face as she looked up at him.

Then for a moment it seemed as if his grey eyes grew larger and larger and drew her nearer and nearer.

She had the strange feeling he was reading her secrets and with a little cry she said:

"No! You have no right to investigate me!"

"I wonder why you are afraid of me doing so."

"If I am, it is because it is late and I am going to bed."

She did not ask herself whether it was too abrupt or

perhaps rude to leave in such a manner, but she was frightened of what he might discover about her.

Because she was also frightened of her own feelings where he was concerned, she moved swiftly across the room and out through the door into the hall without anyone attempting to stop her.

Then she was running up the stairs frantically towards her bedroom.

* * *

The next day Helga when she awoke thought she had been extremely stupid.

How could she have allowed herself to be pressured by the Duke or anybody else? And why had she demonstrated to Virginia her talent for telling fortunes?

Her aunt had warned her that it was not the sort of thing she should do at Rock, and as she felt it all seeping over her she knew she had been very foolish.

"I must behave like a normal, ordinary person, which is all I am required to be," she said, "instead of interfering in the Duke's business affairs or trying to make the American girl happy."

She gave a little sigh, and seeing the sunshine percolating through the sides of the curtains she thought she would look out at the Park first thing in the morning, knowing that the deer under the trees and the swans moving on the lake would be a beautiful sight.

Then as she got out of bed she saw there was a piece of paper near the door.

As she went to pick it up she realised she had forgotten

last night to do as Aunt Millicent had made her promise, and that was to lock her door.

'It was quite unnecessary,' she thought. 'There was certainly nobody drunk at dinner.'

She picked up the piece of paper and walked to the window so that she could read it in the sunlight.

Unfolding it she read:

I shall be riding at six-thirty tomorrow morning, and if you wish to accompany me, meet me in the stables at that time.

R

Helga's heart leapt. Then she looked quickly at the clock on the mantelpiece in case it was too late.

To her joy however it was not yet six o'clock and she hurriedly pulled back the curtains, washed herself in cold water, and started to dress.

The Duke must have recalled their conversation about her old, threadbare riding-habit, she thought, and it was very unlikely that Mr. Vanderfeld would be about at six-thirty, or anybody else in the party for that matter.

When she dressed she thought as she looked at herself in the mirror she was not really smart enough to accompany the Duke of Rocklington.

She then thought it did not matter.

All that was really important was that she would be able to ride one of his superb horses, and it was not likely he would notice her particularly, one way or the other.

When she thought about the Countess of Carrington she thought she must have been very naïve not to realise immediately that she was one of the beautiful Ladies who pursued the Duke.

Her Aunt Millicent had told her how they held his interest for a short time until he became bored with them and looked around for someone else.

Several of the other Ladies in the party were equally attractive.

But it was the Countess who appeared to control everything, and the possessive manner in which she talked to the Duke made quite obvious the part she wished to play in his life.

'I suppose she wants to marry him,' Helga thought.

She knew however that it would be a very great mistake for him to do so, for she would not make him happy.

She was not certain how she knew this, but she thought, beautiful though she was, the Countess had not a kind nature, and the Duke would want as his wife somebody kind, gentle, and understanding.

Here again, why she should think so, she had no idea.

After all, he was so complete in himself, so self-centred and authoritative, that there should be no reason for him to need a woman in the same way as her father did or any other man.

At the same time, she thought, even if he did not know it himself, it was what he needed in his life; somebody who would love him for himself and who would care for him quite apart from Rock and all his other possessions.

'It is not the frame that matters where a person is concerned,' Helga thought, 'it is what the frame contains.'

But for a moment nothing mattered except that he had

asked her to go riding with him, and she thought he was being especially kind to show his pleasure at the way things had passed off last night.

It was obvious that Mr. Vanderfeld had believed the Duke really was secretly engaged, and it was also a relief to know, whatever her father felt, that Virginia had no wish to marry him and was in love with Steve back home on his Ranch.

"It is wonderful . . . wonderful!" Helga told herself.

She hurried down the passages until after losing her way for a few minutes she found a young housemaid who escorted her to a side door by which she could reach the stables.

She was so afraid of being late that she ran to the path twisting between the rhododendron bushes until she reached the cobbled yard.

It was then she saw one of the grooms bringing from its stall a magnificent black stallion, and behind them came the Duke.

Helga ran towards him.

"Thank you for remembering me," she said. "I only hope I have not kept you waiting."

"You are just in time," he said with a smile, "otherwise I would have been sure you were still sleeping and would have gone without you."

"If that had happened, I would have been abjectly miserable when I awoke," Helga replied.

"But as it is, all is well," the Duke said.

A few minutes later they were moving out of the yard, Helga mounted on a horse that was better bred, more spirited, and finer in every way than any horse she had ever ridden before.

Her stepfather's animals had in fact been good hunters and therefore strong and reliable.

But the Duke's horses were like precious stones, each one chosen for its own special points and, Helga knew, schooled by their master because he would trust no one but himself to bring an animal to perfection.

They rode for nearly ten minutes without speaking. Then when they reached open ground the Duke said:

"Let us give the horses their heads, and clear the cobwebs from ours!"

Helga smiled in response. Then they were galloping across the open fields and it was a delight she had not expected, after having run away with only a few pounds in her pocket.

When after a long gallop they drew in their horses the Duke said:

"I was right in thinking you would be an excellent rider!"

"That is the best ride I have ever had!" Helga said, her cheeks glowing. "I have never known such a wonderful horse! I feel he must have been a gift from the gods."

The Duke laughed.

"Perhaps that is what he really is, and of course as you are always telling me about the world beyond this, you must know what you are talking about!"

"Now you are being unkind to me," Helga said. "Actually when I told Miss Vanderfeld's fortune last night I discovered that she is very much in love with a fellow American whom she knows at home. So there is no reason for you to be afraid of her trying to marry you."

"Thank you," the Duke said with a note of sarcasm in his voice.

Helga looked at him a little apprehensively.

"Was that . . . impertinent of me?" she asked.

The Duke laughed again.

"Not exactly impertinent, but somewhat unusual," he said. "But then, Helga, you are a very unusual person and I find it very difficult to make up my mind about you."

"I cannot think of any reason why you should want to," Helga replied, "and I think anybody would feel unusual if they were at Rock."

"Is it the Fairy Tale Castle of your dreams?" the Duke asked.

She nodded before she added:

"And the horses have stepped straight out of a Fairy Story too. They ought to be ridden by the winged messengers of the gods, rather than by us."

"I hope you are not suggesting they will be spirited away from me," the Duke said, "for I should miss them if they were."

"Of course you would," Helga agreed.

Helga thought for a moment, then almost as if she were speaking her thoughts aloud she said:

"You have everything, except of course a wife."

She had spoken more to herself than to him, and she started when the Duke said harshly:

"You are not going to tell me that I should get married? Or do you see it clairvoyantly? If so, I think, Helga, I shall give you a good spanking and send you back to Milly in disgrace."

Helga gave a cry of horror.

"No, please, you must not do that! I am trying to do everything that is right, but I spoke without thinking."

"It is something I do not want to hear," the Duke said. "I am sick of being badgered, pushed, enticed, and pressured into taking a wife!"

"I can understand that," Helga said, "but of course you are so handsome and so important that every woman you meet must want to marry you. You should try to look on it as a compliment rather than a menace."

The Duke threw back his head and laughed.

"Are you now instructing me on how I should behave?"

"Oh, no! I was only thinking that it would be a waste of time your getting angry about something which is quite natural on the part of those people who want to share your life with you, or rather are envious because you have so much."

"That is certainly one way of putting it."

"Perhaps one day it will happen, and then you will find it very wonderful!"

"Stop!" the Duke said sharply. "Stop! You are not going to look at me clairvoyantly and I will not have it—do you hear? I do not want to hear the future. I am perfectly content with the present, and I will not have you or anyone else probing into me, looking for things which are best left unseen!"

As he spoke he touched his horse with his whip and as it sprang forward Helga, realising he was running away, followed him.

It took her some time for her to catch him up, and when she did so she realised with a sense of relief that

94

he was smiling and was not angry, as she had half-feared.

"We must go back," he said, "but I want to warn you that if you behave as a Witch, you may be treated like one."

"Will you drop me in the lake and see if I float, which shows that I am innocent?" Helga asked. "Or shall I be subjected to all the tortures that the Scots inflicted on the Witches and which were horribly cruel?"

"I see you know your history," the Duke said in surprise. "I believe the last Witch who was condemned in this part of the world was stoned to death before she could be properly sentenced for her crimes."

"If that is what you are envisaging for me, I shall have to run away again."

Too late Helga realised what she had said without meaning to, and she might have guessed the Duke would not miss it.

"Again?" he repeated. "So you have run away from something which made you afraid. What was it?"

"I am not going to answer that question," Helga said, "because now you are probing, something which you told me you disliked, and I am afraid of it too."

"I want to help you," the Duke said quietly.

"That is kind of you, and perhaps one day I shall need your help. But for the moment I am quite capable of looking after myself."

"You are sure of that?" the Duke enquired.

"Quite . . . quite sure!" Helga boasted.

chapter five

HELGA drew in her horse and exclaimed:

"That was wonderful! I never knew riding could be so marvellous until I came here!"

"I am glad you feel like that," the Duke replied.

"I suppose," Helga said with a little sigh, "that tomorrow will be the last time I shall ever be able to do this."

As she spoke she was thinking that today was Sunday, and hoping there might be a chance of riding early tomorrow morning before everybody left and the Duke took her back to London.

At the same time she hardly realised she was talking aloud.

She was looking out over the undulating green land to where in the valley below there was a twisting silver stream bordered by willows, and beyond again a fir wood silhouetted against the sky.

It was so lovely, and as the country had always been so much a part of her own life she could hardly bear to think she had to leave it to go back to London.

"So you have been happy here!" the Duke said, and his voice seemed to intrude on her thoughts.

"Very, very happy! How could I be anything else when you have been so kind?"

"That is what I want you to think," he said, "and it is something I want to talk to you about, Helga."

She looked at him questioningly and he asked:

"What plans have you made for when you return to London?"

"As it happens, I have no plans," Helga replied, "but now I have the money you have given me, things are not so frightening as they were before."

"Frightening in what way?"

Quickly Helga remembered that she must not be indiscreet and she answered:

"I do not want to think about it. I just want to be happy while I am here and still living in the dream I stepped into from the moment I saw Rock."

"Dreams come to an end," the Duke said in a practical voice, "and I think, Helga, you should talk to me about your future."

She did not answer, and after a moment he said:

"You are very young and very inexperienced, and if you really intend to go on the stage you will encounter many difficulties and will not know how to cope with them."

"Perhaps it . . . would be a . . . mistake."

"I have never met anyone who is a better actress or performed in a way that was so faultless," the Duke said quietly. "Quite frankly, Helga, I think you are a natural actress—something that only happens once in a blue moon—like Mrs. Siddons, Sarah Bernhardt, and perhaps, if we are thinking of women nearer home—Gertie Miller."

Helga laughed.

She had read in the newspapers what a huge success Gertie Miller was at the Gaiety, and she hoped that when she returned to London she would be able to watch her performance and see her in person.

"I would never aspire to be anyone so famous," she said.

"But you are still ambitious to be an actress," the Duke insisted.

Helga made a little gesture with her gloved hand.

"Not really," she said. "I would much rather live in the country and ride horses."

"You could do that," the Duke said, "but I think if you lived in the country for long you would find it rather dull with no one to admire you in those very pretty and attractive gowns in which, as you are well aware, you look very beautiful."

It was the first compliment he had paid her and Helga looked at him in astonishment.

Then speaking in a different tone of voice he said:

"You told me how poor you were. So who paid for the gown you wore last night and the night before? And your expensive day dresses?"

Helga was so surprised at the way he spoke that she told him the truth.

"Because there was so little time to buy anything before I came to Rock," she said, "and Miss Melrose thought my own clothes unsuitable for the part I was to play, I borrowed them from the Theatre."

The Duke put back his head and laughed.

"That was something that never occurred to me! I have been worrying quite unnecessarily as to who was the lucky man whom you allowed to provide them for you."

"Provide them for me?" Helga echoed. "What a funny idea for you to think a man had paid for my clothes! Of course not!"

The way she spoke in her soft voice made the Duke look at her curiously. Then he said:

"Are you really telling me, Helga, that you have no admirer, no ardent swain who is not pressuring you at the moment?"

Helga was just about to say that was true, when she thought of Bernard Howell and the colour came into her face, but she looked away from the Duke and said nothing.

"Then there is someone!" he said beneath his breath. "I thought it impossible, looking as you do, that there could be no one in your life."

"He is . . . horrible . . . beastly! I do not want to . . . talk about him!" Helga said. "I had . . . forgotten him while I was here . . . because here I know I am . . . safe . . . but when I go . . . back to London . . ."

Her voice trailed away into silence.

The Duke brought his horse nearer to hers, saying as if he wished to reassure himself:

"So this man frightens you! Was it because of him that you ran away?"

Helga nodded.

The conversation brought back all too vividly the terror she had felt when she heard her stepfather agree to her marrying Bernard Howell. It had made her know that she had to escape, she had to hide somewhere where he would be unable to find her.

The Duke was looking at her, seeing her profile with its exquisite little straight nose silhouetted against the green of the trees.

Because she was suddenly conscious of him she turned her face, and he was aware of the terror in her eyes.

"Before you leave tomorrow," the Duke said, "I had intended to talk to you seriously, Helga, about your future. But it is always difficult not to be interrupted in the house, so perhaps this is the moment when I should say what I want to say."

"What is . . . that?" she asked in a low voice.

She was still feeling that Bernard Howell was menacing her, and she could almost feel herself running away from him like a frightened animal while he pursued her relentlessly.

"What I would like to do," the Duke said quietly, "is to look after you and save you from being frightened and worried about earning your own living either on stage or elsewhere."

Helga did not understand what he was saying and after a moment she said:

"I have to find . . . something to do, some sort of . . . work."

"I am trying to tell you that is unnecessary," the Duke said. "I will provide you with horses and a carriage in which you can drive when you go shopping or do anything else when I am not with you. I am sure, Helga, that I could make you very happy, as you would make me."

Now what he was saying seemed to percolate Helga's mind, and after a moment she looked at him in a puzzled way and said:

"I . . . I do not . . . really understand what you are trying to . . . say to me. How could I ride your horses or ride in your carriage unless I was staying here?"

"That would be impossible," the Duke said, "but I own a number of small houses in London and I would give you a very attractive one."

Helga did not speak and he went on:

"But if you really wish to go on the stage, I will make sure you have a good part, either at the Gaiety, or at any other Theatre in which I have a great deal of influence. You will start at the top—I will see to that! But I am still not certain it is the right type of life for you."

"It is very . . . very kind of you," Helga said, "but why should you do all this? It is too much. You are making me feel . . . almost as if I was . . . blackmailing you into being so . . . generous."

The Duke looked at her in astonishment.

He found it incredible that she should really not understand what he was trying to say.

But her eyes were puzzled, and the way she was staring at him convinced him that she was in fact even more innocent than she had appeared to be.

Then it suddenly flashed through his mind that being

such an excellent actress she was deliberately acting the part of a young girl who had really no idea at all of what went on in the fashionable world.

Then again with what he called his "perception" he told himself that she was genuinely bewildered and he said quietly:

"What I am offering you, Helga, is my protection. That is a word you do not understand, but it means exactly what it says, that I will protect you from what is frightening you, I will protect you from being poor and hungry, and I will protect you from having to earn your own living, unless you really want to do so."

"It seems unbelievable that you should do such a thing," Helga replied, "and I assume you would want me to do something in return. When the performance with Mr. Vanderfeld is over, perhaps there will be other ones, but I am sure there are not so many that you think it necessary to . . . spend so much . . . money on . . . me."

There was a faint smile on the Duke's lips as he said:

"Yes, I would want you to do something for me, and it is quite simple—I want you to love me!"

Helga's eyes opened so wide that they seemed to fill her whole face.

"Love you?" she asked beneath her breath. "But that is one thing I was told I must . . . not do."

"Who told you that?" the Duke asked sharply.

"My . . . Miss Melrose. She said it would be very wrong and very stupid of me if I fell in love with you, as so many other women have done, and not only Ladies in your own world but also actresses."

"Milly was quite right," the Duke said, "and it is what I would expect her to say to any young girl coming here

103

to Rock for the first time. But now that I have seen you, Helga, now we have talked to each other, I realise how different you are from most young girls of your age, and certainly very different from the other actresses I have known in the past. I want you to love me, and I want to look after you and make you happy."

As what he was saying seemed to sink slowly into Helga's mind, she knew it meant something very different from what she had expected.

He was asking her to behave like the Gaiety Girls who her aunt had said had fawned on him and did everything in their power to attract his attention.

It was in the same way that the Countess of Carrington and the other beautiful women at Rock appeared to flirt with every word they said to him, their white hands going out to touch him at every opportunity.

"I must not be like that," Helga told herself.

Aloud she said:

"Thank you very ... very much for ... offering to look after me, but I think if I did fall in love with you it might make me ... very unhappy."

"Why should you think that?" the Duke asked truculently.

"Because at the moment love does not play a big part in your life," Helga said, "and love is something which grows and becomes more intense, more wonderful as time goes by ... and ... as you would not ... love me ... it is inevitable that I should feel ... sad and perhaps very ... miserable."

She was thinking it out for herself in a way the Duke had never heard it put before, and he thought how intelligent she was.

At the same time it was not what he wanted to hear.

"Are you really going to refuse to let me look after you, Helga?"

"I would . . . like to say 'yes,'" she answered, "but it would seem part of a . . . Fairy Story that could not be true . . . and I do not think . . . Mama would approve."

"I cannot believe your mother, if she were alive, would approve of your going on the stage either," the Duke said, "unless because you are so attractive it was something she envisaged for you when you were still a child."

"No, of course not. Mama and Papa were very shocked at the idea of the stage."

She was thinking as she spoke of how horrified they had been by her Aunt Millicent's conduct, and how they had always spoken of her with hushed voices as if it were really something they wished to hide.

"What it comes down to," the Duke remarked, working it out, "is that, because you are poor and yet outstandingly pretty, you think the only possible way of earning your living is to go on stage."

"There must be other ways," Helga said, "but I have not really had time to . . . think about . . . them."

"Not since you ran away."

"Yes . . . that is . . . so."

"Then I suggest you should be a great deal more honest with me than you have been up until now and tell me why you have run away and from whom? Then we can decide what it is best for you to do."

"I . . . I cannot tell you that."

"Why not?"

"Because it is too dangerous . . . and also you would not . . . understand."

"Why should you think that? I have always thought of myself as an understanding person."

"I am sure you are, but it is too difficult to explain, except that I came to Rock because Miss Melrose wanted to please you, and I think it would be a mistake to become any further involved than I am at the . . . moment."

"So you admit to being involved? Then let me say, Helga, I find myself very, very involved with you."

Helga was silent, and after a moment he said:

"We must talk about this later today, and for the moment leave things as they are. But before we go back to London tomorrow I want to have everything clear in my mind just in case like a wraith you vanish as suddenly as you appeared and I am left searching for you in a waterless desert."

The way he spoke made Helga laugh and as she touched her horse with her whip and he moved forward, the Duke was obliged to move too.

They rode back through the woods she had visited the previous day and she thought how lovely they were, how enchanted, and how, if she was a wraith or perhaps a nymph she would be able to disappear into the greenery.

Then there would be no more problems, no more difficulties to face.

It was only when she was back at the house and the maid was helping her change from her riding-habit into one of the pretty gowns that had been provided for her by Nellie that she asked herself if she was being very stupid not to accept the Duke's offer.

She was not certain what it really entailed, but he had said he wanted to protect her.

But she was feeling he did not only mean protect her from men like Mr. Howell.

Without really thinking about it she said to the maid:

"Tell me, Mary, what does it mean when a Gentleman offers somebody his protection?"

Her maid, who was a woman of about thirty years of age, looked surprised. Then she said:

"That's not anything that a young Lady like yourself should be talking about!"

"Why not?" Helga asked.

"Because it ain't right, Miss, and it's somethin' bad, if you know what I means."

"Bad?" Helga asked in surprise.

The maid glanced over her shoulder as if to make sure the door of the Bedroom was closed. Then she said:

"It's like this, Miss—there was ever such a pretty young Governess staying here once looking after His Grace's young cousins who'd come here with the rest of the family for Christmas."

The maid glanced over her shoulder again before she lowered her voice and went on:

"We all noticed that Lord Frederick Marsh was always upstairs in the Schoolroom taking an interest in the children!"

Helga looked at her wide-eyed and the maid went on:

"The Housekeeper, when she 'ears about it, says: 'You mark my words, there'll be trouble over this before we're very much older! And there was trouble, Miss, because of what 'appened.'"

"What did happen?" Helga asked.

"When Christmas was over, the Governess, Miss

Cooper was her name, gives in her notice and leaves immediate leavin' the children and Her Ladyship in the lurch. An' why do you think she'd gone?"

"I have no idea," Helga said.

"Because Lord Frederick had offered her his protection, taken her off to London, and given her a smart house in St. John's Wood. One of the menservants at Rocklington House in Grosvenor Square saw her drivin' in the Park, bold as brass, behind two horses with a footman on the box!"

"Do you mean that Lord Frederick had given them to her?"

"Of course, Miss! He was her Protector. We was all shocked that she should have gone off in such a way, not troubling even to give in her month's notice, as she should have done!"

Helga said nothing. She was beginning to suspect now what the Duke was offering her and was as shocked as the maid had been over the Governess.

"It is because he thinks I am an actress," she told herself.

At the same time, she thought, having said so much about his perception he might have been aware that it was something she would not think of doing.

In fact she would sooner starve!

Because now that she understood what he was really suggesting, she wanted to run away from Rock.

She wondered what would happen if she told the maid she had to leave and said she must have a carriage to take her to the nearest Railway Station so that she could go back to London.

Then she remembered if she did that and Mr. Vanderfeld was suspicious that she was not in fact the Duke's *fiancée*, the Duke might stop his cheque and not only would she lose the 1,000 pounds he had given her, but her Aunt Millicent would lose the same amount.

"I have to stay here until tomorrow," Helga decided, "as I have arranged to do. After that I need never see him again."

At the same time, she knew she wanted to see him. She wanted to stay at Rock and ride his horses, to look at the beautiful things in his house, to be surrounded by interesting and exciting people who might have been friends of her father and mother.

Then she knew this was something that would never happen to her again and in the future she would have only her memories of Rock, of how beautiful it was, how elegant the people staying there.

Most of all there would be only memories of the Duke, magnificent and overwhelming.

'I would like to be with him, and I am sure it would be quite easy to fall in love with him,' Helga thought. 'But that is something which must never happen, for if it did, I would become like Aunt Millicent, ostracised and spoken of with lowered voices by everyone who calls themselves "respectable."'

And yet already in the Duke's eyes she was "tarred with the same brush" as her aunt.

She was an actress; she was a woman who could be offered a man's protection, but never anything as stable as marriage.

It struck her, although she had not thought about it until now, that Bernard Howell's offer had been in fact better than that of the Duke's!

Then because she felt as if her thoughts were torturing her, she went downstairs for breakfast to find, as she expected, that the only other Lady present was Virginia Vanderfeld.

Virginia was so thrilled with what Helga had predicted for her that she wanted to talk about the man with whom she was in love, reiterating over and over again how much she missed him.

"Have you seen the Duke's horses?" Helga asked her.

"I'd rather see my own!" Virginia smiled.

Because it was Sunday Helga was determined to go to Church.

She had learned the night before that a carriage for any of the guests who wished to be conveyed to the Church would be waiting outside the front door at a quarter to eleven for the eleven o'clock Service.

She persuaded Virginia rather reluctantly to go with her.

When they got into the carriage it was to find that they were the only two members of the house party who wished to go to the Church.

It was quite near, just outside the gates, and was a very old building mainly Norman with massive pillars and rather beautiful stained-glass west windows which the Duke's grandfather had donated.

To Helga it was very like the little Church she attended in Texas.

Helga found the places for her in the Prayer Book and the Service did not take long.

At the same time Helga prayed fervently that she might be delivered from temptation and not at any time feel like accepting the Duke's proposition.

"If I spend all my money, Mama, it may be difficult to say 'no' when I know how kind and generous he is. But you would not approve, and the only thing I can do is to try to make him understand that I am refusing only because it is wrong, and not because I do not like him."

She felt confused in her mind because the whole thing had been such a shock.

When they drove back to the house with Virginia still talking about the man she was going to marry and the horses she loved in Texas, Helga found herself hoping that the Duke would not be waiting for her to have a further conversation about what they had already discussed.

She tried to keep out of his way, which was easy, for at the moment the Countess of Carrington came downstairs and made it quite clear that her place was beside the Duke and the Duke's beside her.

He had arranged for most of his guests to drive in a variety of carriages to where there was a "Folly" in about the centre of his Estate.

"There is a fine view from the top of it," he said, "and also its architecture is unique. I know Mr. Vanderfeld will enjoy seeing it."

To Helga's relief she did not drive alone with the Duke as she had half-expected might be necessary, if only to continue to deceive Mr. Vanderfeld.

They all four went together, the two men sitting up in front with the Duke driving the extra large Chaise and the two girls sitting behind.

Looking at the back of his head and his square shoulders which seemed broader than any other man's, Helga told herself that even with his back to her he was still the most attractive man she had ever seen.

He drove of course superbly, and when they reached the Folly it was to find it was a strange, tall building with a twisting staircase inside which led out onto a small platform from which, as the Duke had said, there was a spectacular view over the surrounding countryside.

Helga and Virginia climbed to the top and to her surprise after they had been there for a few minutes they were joined by the Duke and Mr. Vanderfeld.

"It's a good thing I'm fit and healthy," the latter observed. "Those stairs are steep enough to give any man who is not healthy a heart attack!"

"That is certainly something you must not have," the Duke replied. "You cannot be spared at this moment, if at any other!"

Mr. Vanderfeld laughed.

"If you are thinking of our deal, Duke, everything should be signed and sealed within the next few days."

They drove back the same way they had come and the Duke explained to Mr. Vanderfeld some of the unusual objects to be found on his Estate and made it clear how well it was organised.

"I shall be waiting for you to come to Texas; Duke," Mr. Vanderfeld said. "Then I can show you how I manage on a very larger amount of land than you own here."

"I am sure I will find it most interesting," the Duke replied in a voice which told Helga it was the last thing he was likely to do.

Mr. Vanderfeld was pleased and when they got back to the house he showed a new enthusiasm for inspecting the house and seeing the pictures.

After a little while, Helga wandered away on her own

and finding herself in the Music Room wondered if she dared to play on the very large and impressive piano that stood on a small dais flanked by Ionic pillars.

Just then the Duke came into the room.

"I thought perhaps I might find you here," he said. "I am sure you are thinking that as this room is perfectly built for it, I should give a Concert, or better still, produce a Play which will amuse my guests."

"Would it amuse you?" Helga asked.

"Certainly, if you were playing the main part," the Duke replied.

There was a note in his voice which made her nervous, and as he came nearer to her she put out her hand onto the piano as if for support.

"Have you been thinking about what I said to you this morning?" he asked.

"Yes . . . I have."

"Then I hope you are going to give me the answer I want."

There was a definite pause before Helga said:

"Please . . . I do not want Your Grace to be . . . angry with me . . . but it is something . . . I cannot do."

"Why not?"

"Because I would feel it was . . . wrong . . . very wrong . . . perhaps the right word is 'wicked'!"

The Duke stared at her in sheer astonishment.

"Do you really mean that?" he asked.

"I was thinking about it today in Church," Helga said. "I knew that I would be . . . sinning if I accepted the . . . protection of a . . . man and . . . loved him without the . . . blessing of God."

She did not look at the Duke as she spoke, and her

voice came rather fitfully from between her lips because she was shy and also frightened.

Then he asked:

"Are you really saying this to me, and it is not just an act?"

"Of course . . . not!"

"Then why are you so determined, to put it bluntly, to be respectable? How can you be contemplating even for a moment taking up a career which is, to say the least of it, very unsuitable for such sentiments?"

"It is difficult to know . . . what to do," Helga said, "but there is now no . . . need for me to make up my . . . mind immediately."

"Because you have the money I have given you?" the Duke asked. "That is all very well, but you must realise it will not last forever, unless you are hoping some very suitable husband will materialise from nowhere who is prepared, which I think is unlikely, to accept an actress as his wife. Then you are going to find that inevitably you will be looking around for a Protector."

His voice changed as he said quietly and beguilingly:

"I would like to be the first man in your life, Helga, and if you would only trust me, I think it would be a very, very long time before either of us would wish to part from the other."

As the Duke spoke he came a little nearer to her and Helga knew that she had to move only a few inches, or perhaps he would, for her to be in his arms.

It flashed through her mind that if he held her close against him she would feel safe and would no longer be afraid.

When she thought of it a sensation she did not understand seemed to tingle through her and she felt as if it were a ray of sunshine through her body.

Quite suddenly she was afraid, desperately afraid, not of the Duke, but of herself.

She was afraid to give in to him, of doing what she knew was wrong and would horrify her mother, just because he was so attractive.

With a little cry that seemed to echo around the Music Room she turned, and as his arms went out to stop her from leaving she slipped away from him.

Then she ran across the polished floor and out into the passage.

Now she was running faster than she had ever run in her life before through the hall and up the stairs to her Bedroom.

Only as she reached it did she realise that this was the first time since she had been at Rock that she had wanted to lock the door.

It was not so much against the Duke, as against her own feelings, which she found uncontrollable.

* * *

Helga stayed in her Bedroom until it was nearly five o'clock.

Then she had a longing to be outside in the open air and an even greater one to go riding.

She had heard somebody say that dinner would be late tonight and they would not be dining until half-past-eight.

That gave her plenty of time, she thought, for an hour's ride, and quickly she put on her riding-habit.

Going down the back stairs so that no one would see her, she let herself out by the same door she had used in the morning which took her to the stables.

One of the grooms saw her approaching and asked:

"Ye're goin' fer a roide, Miss?"

"If you will find me a horse," Helga answered.

"No difficulty about that, Miss."

He went down the stables and came back with what she thought was an even finer animal than the one she had ridden in the morning.

It took him only a minute to put on the side-saddle, and then as she mounted from the mounting-block the groom asked:

"Ye'll be roidin' alone, Miss?"

"Yes, alone!" Helga said firmly, and tried not to wish with all her heart that the Duke were with her.

She rode off in a different direction from the way she had gone that morning.

Only as she found herself in another part of the estate did she remember that the Duke had said casually at luncheon that there was to be a Horse Sale on one part of his estate the following day.

"Is there anything worth buying, Hugo?" one of his friends asked.

"I should not imagine so," the Duke replied. "One or two of the local farmers and Squires have some quite good hunters, but I suspect that you and I would be better served by going to Tattersall's."

"That is what I thought," was the reply, "but I might have a look at what there is before I leave. I presume I can stay until after luncheon?"

"Of course," the Duke agreed, "and I might come

116

with you. One never knows—sometimes one finds the most outstanding horse in the most unlikely of places."

Both the men had laughed.

When Helga saw in the distance that a marquee had been erected near a farmhouse and in front of it posts and rails forming a ring, she knew what it meant.

Because she was curious she rode towards it, feeling there were not likely to be many horses yet on view and most of them would be arriving the following morning.

"But tomorrow I am leaving," she told herself as she went.

Insidiously, because she could not help herself, the thought of an alternative entered her mind, which was to do as the Duke required of her and let him be her Protector.

"It is wrong, wrong, wrong!" she told herself.

But somehow there was not as much conviction in the words as there had been earlier in the day.

chapter six

HELGA rode on, and as she drew nearer to the Horse Show she saw that there were already quite a number of horses being led out of the horse boxes in which they had obviously recently arrived.

Because she was always thrilled by horse flesh she felt curious and also wondered if by any chance there was the sort of animal which the Duke would think good enough for his stables.

It was unlikely. At the same time she thought it would be rather fun if she could tell him she had found a horse he might like.

There was a young chestnut horse bucking and kicking and obviously upset by his journey.

The groom who had travelled with him was having the greatest difficulty in keeping a hold of the bridle and at the same time keeping himself out of the way of the flying hoofs.

She watched with interest and then as he was gradually brought under control she looked around to see there was by now a number of horses walking around the ring, no doubt being rehearsed for their appearance tomorrow.

She rode nearer to them, and as she was watching a rather nice-looking bay her attention was distracted by a man shouting angrily at a boy who was opening the door of a horse box.

There was something hard and ugly in the tone of his voice, and she also realised as she listened that he was using a number of swear words which were not those she had ever heard before.

Then as she looked at him, thinking how unpleasant he was, her heart leapt with fear. He had had his back to her, but now he turned round to ride towards the ring and as he did so, he saw her.

It was then that Helga realised she was looking at Bernard Howell and for a moment she was completely paralysed with horror.

Then with a cry of sheer terror she turned her horse and started to ride away.

As she did so, she heard Bernard Howell call her name:

"Helga! Helga! I want to speak to you!"

He spoke in a loud voice which she could hear quite clearly.

Then as she rode on, urging her horse to move even faster, incredulously she heard him shout:

"Tally-ho! Gone away!"

A moment later she heard the sound of a hunting horn.

She knew he habitually carried one in the inside pocket of his coat, an affectation which proclaimed to all and sundry what an experienced huntsman he was.

Now, as she was aware he was pursuing her, her dream in which she had thought of herself as a fox with Bernard Howell in full chase after her had come true.

She rode blindly towards a wood that was on one side of the field.

Then as she entered it she realised she had made a mistake and being in the wood slowed her progress.

It would slow him too, but as a low branch knocked her riding-hat from her head she forced herself to subdue her blind panic and think a little more clearly.

She twisted in and out of the trees, knowing that behind her and gaining ground was Bernard Howell.

Then thankfully she emerged on to the ride and was aware as she started to gallop down it that it would carry her out on the other side of the wood into open ground.

Riding more swiftly than she had ever done in her life before, she had almost reached the end of the ride when she heard Bernard Howell's voice in the distance and knew he had seen her.

"Tally-ho! Gone away!" he shouted, and then again there was the sound of the hunting horn.

"Save me! Oh, God, save me!" Helga prayed.

She knew as she did so the only person who could help her would be the Duke.

*   *   *

The Duke had, after tea, left his house party and gone to his private Study.

There were, he knew, many letters to be signed and he also wanted to be alone to think about Helga.

He was, in fact, completely disconcerted by the way she had taken his proposal that he should look after her.

It was the first time in his life than any woman to whom he had offered his protection had told him firmly that such an idea was wrong and wicked.

"How can she possibly think such a thing?" he asked himself. "If she takes up a stage career, it is inevitable that sooner or later she will need some man to pay her bills and dress her to show off to its best advantage her beauty."

It was common knowledge that not a single actress in the Gaiety did not supplement her salary by accepting gifts from her admirers.

In fact it would have been impossible for them to pay the rent of any comfortable flat without such assistance.

"She must have some knowledge of the profession she is entering," the Duke argued to himself.

He wondered once again if Helga's protestations of her innocence were really a clever act put on for his benefit.

And yet he would have sworn that she was completely genuine and that the idea of living with a man without marriage did sincerely shock her.

'Milly must have told her something about life on the stage,' he thought irritably.

He found himself wondering with a curiosity which increased all the time as to where Milly could have found someone so unique and at such short notice.

Unable to sit at his desk, he walked restlessly across the Study thinking about Helga.

He had tried to catch her out in her professed knowledge of pictures only to find that she really did know a great deal about them and even about architecture also.

In fact, he thought, if he had met her in the ordinary course of his social life, he would have considered her very well read and obviously expensively educated.

Yet Helga had told him that her parents were very poor, and if nothing else, her riding-habit was proof of this and was, the Duke knew, in urgent need of replacement.

He thought of Helga as being dressed in a habit made by Busuine which would display her figure to its very best advantage, with boots from Maxwell's on her small feet, and a riding-hat from Lock's.

"She would look sensational in any hunting field," he told himself.

Then he remembered that Helga had made it absolutely clear that she would not allow any man to pay for her clothes.

"Dammit all, the girl has to wake up to reality!" he muttered. "She will find sooner or later that she has made a great mistake in refusing me!"

Then the thought of somebody else draping sables over Helga's white shoulders or putting jewels round her long, slim neck made him frown and feel like clenching his fists.

How could he let her go back to London, knowing that even with the thousand pounds he had given her to come to Rock she would find it impossible to look after herself.

How would she cope with the "stage-door Johnnies" who could be very persuasive and make themselves very tiresome if they wished to get to know a new star in the theatrical firmament.

As he thought of the way some of the elegant young "men-about-town" behaved, and as he remembered the fear he had seen in Helga's eyes, the Duke asked himself almost despairingly what he could do about it.

He could not believe for a moment that she intended to go on refusing him, and yet he had the uncomfortable feeling that he was up against something he had never encountered before in all the women he had pursued, and that was quite simply—purity.

That Helga was physically pure at the moment went without saying, but his perception told him that it went far deeper than that.

What she had was a purity of mind, heart, and soul, and that was something that might prove itself a rock on which he could beat himself unavailingly.

"What can I do about her?" he asked aloud.

It did not enter his mind that it was the first time in his life that he had felt seriously perturbed about any woman or that she caused him so much anxiety that he was uncharacteristcally unsure of himself and of the next move he should make.

He walked up and down the Study, then went to the window to look out on the shadows that were growing longer in the garden and in the Park beyond the lake.

Then to his astonishment he saw a woman, and he realised at once that it was Helga, coming "hell-for-leather" through the trees at the top of the Park and riding at breakneck speed between the great oaks towards the house.

His first thought was one of consternation because it

was clear to him that something had upset her.

His second that she was taking a foolhardy risk in galloping over ground that was full of rabbit holes which might cause her horse to fall at any moment and fling her over its head.

Then as he watched her, thinking it was unlike her to take such risks and it was the first time he had ever known her break the rules which every good rider followed, that he saw there was a man riding behind her.

The man was beating his horse violently in an effort to increase its speed and was riding over the rough ground in the same reckless way that Helga was doing.

The Duke realised that while Helga was riding one of his best horses, the man pursuing her was compelling his horse by sheer cruelty to move faster and still faster in his efforts to catch her.

Then to his astonishment he heard the sound of the hunting horn, saw who was blowing it, and as Helga crossed the bridge over the lake, he heard the man shout:

"I have got you now, my pretty vixen!"

Helga did not turn her head, but merely rode as swiftly as she could up to the front door, and without even waiting for the groom who was always in attendance for anyone out riding, slipped down from his back and ran into the house.

The Duke lingered a moment to see what the man following her would do.

He saw that as he reached the steps which led up to the front door he too swung himself from his saddle.

Then as he did so the Duke heard footsteps running down the passage outside his room and a second later the door opened and Helga came in.

One glance at her was enough to tell him how terrified she was.

For the first time since he had seen her on a horse she looked untidy, hatless, her hair curling riotously over her forehead and round the sides of her cheeks.

She rushed across the room towards him and putting out her hands to hold on to him gasped in a voice that was so breathless it was hardly audible:

"S-save me . . . save me . . . he will . . . t-take me away . . . and I shall . . . have to . . . m-marry him! Hide me . . . please . . . hide me!"

Her voice broke on the words and, as the Duke put out his hands to support her in case she should fall to the ground, he heard through the door which she had left ajar, a man's voice talking loudly at the end of the passage.

"Hide . . . me!" Helga gasped again.

The Duke looked around the Study as if he were seeing it for the first time.

On one side of the fireplace was an armchair in which his father had always sat and which because he had complained of a draught had a heavy leather screen arranged protectively behind it.

Without saying anything the Duke drew Helga quickly across the room, and when he took her to the side of the screen which almost touched the wall by the mantelpiece she saw an aperture and slipped through it, being then hidden completely from anybody who was in the Study.

The Duke then walked to his desk and seating himself took up his pen and started studying the papers which had been piled by his secretary on top of the blotter.

It was only a few seconds before the door opened and one of the footmen looking startled said:

"There's a gentleman wishes to see Your Grace."

"I am too busy to see anyone!" the Duke said sharply.

"You will see me!"

Pushing past the footman Bernard Howell came into the room.

The Duke looked up with an expression of well-simulated surprise on his face at the intrusion.

As he looked up at the fat, red-faced man, who it was obvious habitually drank too much, he could understand why Helga was afraid.

"I am not receiving visitors at the moment," he said coldly.

Quite unabashed, Bernard Howell walked up to the desk and facing the Duke said:

"I have come, Your Grace, to claim something which belongs to me, and which is attempting to avoid me by taking refuge in your house!"

"I have not the slightest idea what you are talking about," the Duke said.

"I cannot believe that," Bernard Howell said. "The young woman who was riding one of your horses ran in through your front door as if she were by no means a stranger, and I understand from your servants that she is, in fact, staying with you."

"Since you appear to be so well-informed," the Duke said, "perhaps we should start at the beginning. First kindly tell me who you are and by what right you come storming into my private room without my permission!"

A lesser man would have been crushed by the note

127

in the Duke's voice, but Bernard Howell, without being invited, sat down on a chair by the Duke's desk and said:

"My name is Bernard Howell. I come from Worcestershire, where I am well known in sporting circles."

The Duke's eyes flickered over the whip Howell was carrying in one hand and rested for an instant on the hunting horn which he could see just beneath the revere of his coat.

He did not speak and Bernard Howell went on;

"Helga Wensley, whom I have just seen entering your house, is to be my wife."

He paused, then as if he anticipated the Duke might deny there was anyone of that name staying with him, he said:

"As she ran away from home to hide herself in this reprehensible fashion, she is doubtless using a false name, but she is in reality, Your Grace, the Honourable Helga Wensley, daughter of the late Lord Wensley and stepdaughter of Sir Hector Preston who, as her legal Guardian, has given his consent to our marriage."

"If Miss Wensley has run away from you," the Duke said slowly, "it does not sound as if she is very enthusiastic about the union."

"That is immaterial!" Bernard Howell said. "As Your Grace must be aware, a Guardian has complete control over his Ward, and Sir Hector Preston wishes his stepdaughter to marry me."

"A very interesting story," the Duke said quietly. "What do you expect me to do about it?"

"I expect Your Grace to hand over Miss Wensley to me immediately, when I will take her home and ensure

128

that this sort of thing does not happen again."

"And how do you propose to achieve that?" the Duke asked, a faint note of amusement in his voice.

Bernard Howell's eyes narrowed.

"I assure Your Grace that I know how to treat a disobedient horse and a disobedient young woman! It may be a painful process, but Helga Wensley will learn obedience, which is what I expect from my wife."

The way he spoke made the Duke long to smash his fist into the man's complacent face, but he merely said with an air of indifference:

"I am afraid what you ask, Mr. Howell, is not possible!"

"What do you mean—not possible?" Bernard Howell enquired.

"Exactly what I say," the Duke replied. "It is not possible for Miss Wensley, as you call her, to leave here at this particular moment."

Bernard Howell bent forward in his chair.

"Now, look here, Your Grace, I know the law, and it is on my side. Helga Wensley comes away with me immediately, or I will get from the Magistrates an Injunction against you for abducting a minor."

The way he spoke was intimidating, but the Duke merely looked at him contemptuously.

"If you know the law, Mr. Howell, so do I, and as an employer I have my rights. A contract of employment has to be completed before the worker concerned is free to leave."

"Worker?" Bernard Howell exclaimed. "Are you telling me that Helga is working for you?"

"Miss Wensley undertook to serve me in a certain capacity for which she has been paid. Until that work is completed I will not allow her to leave."

"And when will that be?"

"Tomorrow afternoon, when I shall take her back to London," the Duke replied.

"In that case," Bernard Howell said, "I must concede that for the moment your jurisdiction over her must stand. But I expect, Your Grace, to pick her up tomorrow afternoon, and you will tell me where I can do so."

"Certainly," the Duke replied. "Shall we say at four o'clock at my house in Grosvenor Square?"

Bernard Howell rose to his feet.

"I will wait until then, but I expect you to tell Helga that I will not stand for any more of her tricks, and if she runs away again, she will sorely regret it."

There was a threat in Bernard Howell's voice that the Duke did not miss, and almost as if he wished to emphasise what he had said, he slapped his riding-whip hard against one of his highly polished boots.

"Four o'clock tomorrow afternoon, Your Grace," he said, "and if Miss Wensley is not available, I shall apply immediately for an Injunction."

"You have made that very clear, Mr. Howell," the Duke said, "and now, as I am extremely busy—good afternoon!"

Bernard Howell did not reply. He merely walked from the room, closing the door noisily behind him.

The Duke waited without moving until his footsteps could not longer be heard going down the passage.

Only then did he rise to his feet and walk across to

130

the fireplace to draw aside the heavy leather screen behind which Helga had been hiding.

He had somehow expected her to rush out and hold on to him as she had done before, but instead she came out very slowly and he saw her face was ashen white.

"It is all right," the Duke said. "He has gone."

"Until . . . tomorrow!" she whispered.

"By that time we can think of what we can do," the Duke said, "and do not be afraid. I will . . ."

At that moment the door opened and Mr. Vanderfeld came into the Study.

"I've been looking for you, Duke," he said, "because I have to tell you that a Courier has just arrived from London to inform me that it is of the utmost urgency that I go to London to attend a Board Meeting that is taking place tomorrow morning at nine o'clock."

He did not seem to notice Helga standing at the Duke's side.

Seeming impressed by the importance of what he had to impart, Mr. Vanderfelt went on:

"I hope therefore Your Grace will understand if I leave tonight immediately after dinner for a train which I understand can be stopped at your private Halt just before ten o'clock. I have learnt it will get me to London in under an hour. Then there will be no need for me to miss the meeting tomorrow. I feel sure you will understand."

"Of course I understand," the Duke said. "I am only sorry that your visit to Rock has to be cut short."

As he spoke he was aware that Helga with the swiftness of a frightened animal had slipped from the room and he and Mr. Vanderfeld were alone.

By the time he had listened to what the American had to say and he was very voluble on the importance of the meeting which required his presence, the Duke was sure that Helga would have gone upstairs to her room.

There would therefore be no opportunity for them to talk any further before dinner.

He wondered if it would be possible for him to send for her, or to ask to meet him before the party gathered in the Silver Salon as they had last night.

Then, while he was thinking about it, the Countess of Carrington came into the Study and Mr. Vanderfeld left.

She was even more voluble than the American, on the subject of how the Duke was neglecting her.

It had been a miserable weekend as far as she was concerned because she had seen so little of him.

The Duke was used to his love affairs coming to an abrupt end, and finding that being bored with a woman, he really had no wish to see her again.

He had however not suspected that his relationship with the Countess had reached that stage until he found himself so intrigued and curious about Helga.

Then she had, in an astonishing way, completely held his attention.

He had hardly listened while the Countess talked to him at meals, and had avoided, with an adroitness learnt by experience, being alone with her at other times.

He knew that what had really infuriated her was that he had not come as she expected to her Bedroom after everybody had retired to bed.

He had slept in his own room and made no explanation of having done so the following day.

"We have been so happy together, Hugo," the Count-

132

ess said now, looking extremely alluring in a green gown which mirrored the green of her slanting eyes. "How can you be so unkind as to leave me to play hostess to your friends while you disappear?"

"I have had a lot to do," the Duke said vaguely, "and as you are well aware, the party was given for Mr. Vanderfeld and I had to look after him."

"I have just learned that he is leaving after dinner," the Countess said. "That means that at least you will be free of him tonight."

It is quite obvious there was a deeper meaning behind her words, and there was a hint of fire in her eyes which the Duke had seen on many previous occasions.

She moved a little nearer to him to touch his cheek with her long fingers.

"I love you, Hugo," she said softly, "and when you are not in my arms kissing me, I find everything else a great waste of time."

"Time is always in short supply when one has a house party," the Duke answered, "and you must therefore forgive me, Betty, if we postpone this conversation until I have less to do."

The Duke disentangled himself from the Countess's arms and moved towards the door.

"I must see that the carriage has been ordered so that Mr. Vanderfeld can catch his train," he said, "and I think it would be polite if I accompanied him to the station."

"Really, Hugo, that is surely quite unnecessary . . . ?" the Countess began, only to find that the Duke had already gone and she was alone in the Study.

She gave a cry of sheer exasperation and stamped her foot with fury at the Duke's elusiveness.

It never entered her mind that he was in fact tired of her, and that, although she had no idea of it, this would be the last time she would see him alone.

*   *   *

As the Duke dressed for dinner he planned what he would say to Helga and was determined that somehow he would get her alone when everybody else was playing cards.

As she was one of his least important guests she was seated far away down the end of the table away from him at dinner.

And yet he found himself watching her.

She was very pale, and he knew if he were near enough to her, he would see the fear behind her eyes.

She appeared to be very quiet, but nevertheless was behaving in a circumspect and courageous way which he admired.

Most women in her position at the moment would, he knew, be having hysterics, clinging to some man, crying on his shoulder, and reiterating over and over again how frightened they were.

He was well aware that Helga was frightened and that she had every reason for it.

It struck him for the first time that she was behaving like the Lady she was by birth, and now he understood a great many things that had puzzled him.

She was not an actress and never had been, and it must have been simply because she needed the money that she had agreed to play the part he required of her.

But why, when she had run away from that impossible man Howell, had she gone to Milly?

134

It was then that the Duke guessed the truth. Christopher Forsythe who was a close friend of his had confided in him years ago who Milly really was and he knew if he looked up her father in Burke's *Country Gentlemen* he would find that he had another daughter who must have married Lord Wensley.

Helga was Milly's niece. That would account for her being available and being exactly the person he wanted to play the part of his *fiancée* for the benefit of Mr. Vanderfeld.

The Duke knew a feeling of elation at having solved what had seemed a baffling puzzle, and he longed to talk it over with Helga to make sure that he was right and to find out exactly how everything had fallen into place.

Then to his consternation, when the Gentlemen left the Dining Room to join the Ladies in the Silver Salon and the Countess swept towards him and her hands were touching him, there was no sign of Helga.

The Duke was aware that it would be a great mistake to ask Betty Carrington, who he knew was exceedingly jealous, what had happened to his youngest and most unimportant guest.

He therefore had to wait for nearly half an hour before a footman told him that the carriage was at the door and Mr. Vanderfeld and his daughter were about to come downstairs.

The Duke went out to the hall to meet the Vanderfelds who had gone upstairs immediately dinner was finished to change into travelling clothes.

"I will come to see you off," he said.

"No, no, I wouldn't hear of it, Duke!" Mr. Vanderfeld said. "You must stay with your guests. I am sorry we have to disrupt the party by leaving in this precipitate manner, but, as you know, business is business, and it takes precedence over everything else."

"Of course you are right," the Duke agreed.

He did however make another effort to accompany the Vanderfelds but they would not hear of it.

Only as they walked to the front door was the Duke able to say to Virginia:

"Have you said good-bye to Miss Grosvenor?"

"Yes, but then she went upstairs to bed while I changed for the journey. She said she had a headache."

"I am sorry to hear that," the Duke said conventionally.

Then Mr. Vanderfeld was saying once again how much he and Virginia had enjoyed their visit, and how much he was looking forward to meeting him again in London.

"I am bringing Potter over with me to Grosvenor Square," Mr. Vanderfeld said. "I am very eager for you to meet him."

"I shall be looking forward to it," the Duke replied.

Then the comfortable carriage with two well-matched horses drove off and he waved from the steps before he turned and went back into the hall.

It was infuriating to think he had missed seeing Helga.

It flashed through his mind that he might go later to her Bedroom and talk to her, because he was quite certain she would not be asleep but worrying about her future.

Then he told himself that if he did that, she would undoubtedly be very shocked, and once again he was up against a barrier of purity that he had never met in anybody else.

The evening seemed to drag on slowly and for the Duke it was extremely boring.

The Countess tried with every wile in her repertoire to entice him into playing Roulette with her, or talking to her intimately on one of the sofas.

Somehow he avoided being snared, and after two rubbers of Bridge, which he lost because he could not give the cards his full attention, to his relief the party began to break up.

It seemed to the Duke to take an unconscionably long time for them all to discuss the weekend and say good night to each other.

Finally however they walked slowly up the magnificent staircase towards their bedrooms.

His valet was waiting for him, and once again when the man had left him alone the Duke wondered whether it would be possible for him to talk to Helga.

Then he looked at the clock to see it was getting on for half-past-twelve and knew it was quite impossible for him to wake her, if she was asleep, or upset her by his sudden appearance, if she was not.

If it had been any other woman, he knew he would not have hesitated, and if it had been somebody like Betty Carrington, he would have been welcomed with open arms whatever time of the night he called on her.

Helga was different and he was quite certain that if he did try to see her she would either refuse to let him stay or else be frightened, because she thought it was wrong and unconventional.

"No wonder she did not understand when I offered to

take her under my protection!" the Duke told himself with a twist of his lips.

Then it struck him that in the circumstances she might accept his suggestion rather than endure the cruelty she would receive at the hands of Bernard Howell as his wife.

The Duke had not missed the way in which he talked of extorting obedience from his horses and his women.

Being a good judge of men, he knew that Howell was a brute and a bully, and Helga had done the only thing possible in running away from him.

"How could her stepfather expect her to marry a man like that?" he asked himself.

He found it difficult to wait until tomorrow when he would see her and find out all the details of a story that grew even more intriguing every minute he thought about it.

At the same time he was well aware, and it was horrifying to think of it, that Howell had the law on his side.

If it was true, and there was no reason to think it was not, that Helga's stepfather had agreed to their marriage, there was nothing he or anybody else could do about it.

"I have to save her," the Duke told himself.

He however had no idea how he could do so without having Howell's hands at his throat.

The man had already threatened to take out an Injunction against him, and he felt sure it was something he would take great pleasure in doing.

At the same time it was unthinkable that Helga, so innocent, so sensitive, should marry a man who would treat her with physical cruelty and most likely destroy her mentally.

"What am I to do? What the devil am I to do?" the Duke asked when finally he got to bed to lay awake in the darkness.

The whole story seemed to be twisting and turning in his mind, but he could find no answer to his question.

He was in fact, almost dropping off to sleep when something disturbed him.

It was not a noise, it was as if perceptively he was aware that somebody was near him.

He could not explain it to himself, because there seemed no reason for him to feel suddenly alert.

And yet he knew that he was awake and that it was almost as if he was being warned.

But warned of what?

'I am letting my imagination run away with me,' the Duke thought.

Then because he felt uncontrollably restless, he got out of bed and drew back the curtains to let in some air through an open casement.

Outside the moonlight was turning the garden and the Park into a Fairyland of silver beauty.

The stars glittered overhead and everything looked enchanted.

The Duke could see only two large, frightened eyes looking at him appealingly and it was as if Helga were beside him, begging him to help her.

"Dammit all!" he expostulated. "I have to see her!" It is better for her to be shocked by me than to suffer as I know she is doing at the moment."

139

Resolutely he walked towards the door and as he did so he saw there was a small piece of paper showing underneath it.

For a moment he stared at it incredulously.

Then he bent down and picked it up.

chapter seven

THE Duke lit the candle beside his bed and opened the piece of paper.

As he did so he felt that to read it gave him a physical pain.

> *There is nothing else I can do. Please make everybody think it was an accident. I told my maid while I was dressing that I often go for a walk at night if I cannot sleep. You have been so kind and I must not hurt you, which I would do if you tried to hide me.*
>
> *Thank you, thank you for everything!*
> *Helga.*

The Duke stared at the piece of paper as if he could not believe what was written there.

Then with the swiftness of a man who has been used to danger, he pulled open his wardrobe, put on a shirt and the first pair of trousers he came to.

Then tying a silk scarf round his neck he ran down the passage and down a side staircase which led to one of the doors into the garden.

He pulled back the bolts and once outside started to run more quickly than he had ever done since his school-days at Eton.

It was his instinctive sense that told him exactly where Helga had gone, and he could remember saying to her when they were riding alongside the lake:

"I used to swim here when I was a boy."

"Is it something you do now?" she had enquired.

"Not as often as I would like," the Duke confessed. "The lake has got rather shallow except at the far end where it is still very deep. The gardeners think it is dangerous, although I suspect they exaggerate."

As what he had said came back to him he could see Helga listening, her large eyes looking into his intently.

He was sure that was what she would have remembered, and as he sped through the gardens, then through the orchard that bordered the lake at the far end, he was praying as he had not prayed for many years that he would not be too late.

The moonlight illuminated everything, and yet it also cast frightening dark shadows that seemed to loom up in his path almost like menacing monsters.

Conscious that his heart was beating frantically and his breath was coming in gasps between his lips, he reached a clump of bushes that grew alongside the lake and saw to his unutterable relief a slim body standing silhouetted against the moonlit water.

He was in time, but only just, because as he reached Helga he realised as he put out his hands towards her that her body was tense.

She had been at that very second about to spring forward into the deep water.

As he caught hold of her she gave a little scream of fear.

Then as she realised who he was she cried:

"No . . . no . . . you must not stop me . . . there is . . . nothing else I can do . . . but die!"

The Duke pulled her close against him before in a voice that did not sound like his own, he demanded:

"How could you do anything so wrong, so wicked as to throw away your life?"

"I have to . . . do you not . . . understand? I have to!" Helga cried. "If you hide me . . . Mr. Howell will accuse you of . . . doing so . . . and there will be a scandal in which you will be . . . involved and . . . wherever I go . . . he will pursue me."

Her voice came in uneven gasps and the Duke, pulling her even more closely to him, said:

"I am not at all afraid of Mr. Howell, and I cannot allow you to do anything so abominable as to drown yourself."

She did not answer but he felt her body relax against him and was aware that she was wearing nothing but her nightgown and a muslin negligée.

Then in a more gentle tone he said:

"You have been so brave, you must not give in now."

"I am . . . not brave," Helga said, and now her voice was little more than a whisper. "I . . . I am a coward . . . and I am afraid . . . I am . . . afraid of his beating me as he beats his horses . . . I could not . . . bear it! Oh . . . please . . . please . . . let me die!"

Her voice broke until suddenly she was crying tumultuously against him.

She wept like a child, with the tears rolling down her cheeks, and the Duke could feel them soaking through his lawn shirt onto his skin.

"I am so afraid . . . so . . . afraid!" she murmured.

The Duke knew that she was past listening to anything he could say while the tempest of her tears swept over her, and he could only hold her close.

As he did so he realised incredibly that he had fallen in love.

It was not love as he had known it in the past, and he knew that what he felt for Helga was very different from what he had felt for any other woman.

He wanted to protect her, to look after her, at whatever cost to himself.

He could feel his heart beating against hers, and he knew that the throbbing in his temples and the feeling of breathlessness in his throat was because Helga was a woman and he was a man.

At the same time it was different, very different from any feeling which he had thought was love and had felt for other women.

Then there had been a fiery exchange between them, a rising irresistible passion which had swept away any other feelings.

What he felt for Helga was a tenderness which was

144

so utterly different that he knew now it had blinded him to the realisation that it was love.

Because she was so innocent, so pure in every way, she had not aroused in him the hungry desire he had in the past always associated with sensations of love.

Instead, he knew that she had crept into his heart so that he was unaware of it until the moment when he thought he might lose her, and knew if he did, he would have lost something so precious that it would have been irreplaceable in his life.

"I love you, my darling, and I will never let you be afraid again," he wanted to say.

But while she cried in his arms he knew she would not hear him or understand.

Instead, he gently kissed the top of her head and knew that his arms gave her a feeling of safety and comfort.

Only as her tears abated a little did he say gently:

"I think we should move away from the edge of the lake. If you fall in now, I shall fall with you, and I have no wish at this particular moment for a cold bath!"

There was a little pause and he knew she was trying to force herself to answer him.

Then she said, a catch in her voice:

"Y-you would be...wise to go away and...leave me...I cannot swim!"

"But I can," the Duke replied, "and I have no wish to play the hero and pull you out!"

As he spoke he led her back from the edge of the lake away from the bushes until they were illuminated by the moonlight.

The Duke looked down at her and thought that with the tear stains on her cheeks, her eyelashes wet with tears, she was still lovelier than anyone he had ever seen.

At the same time she looked so pathetic that she tugged at his heartstrings.

He stood looking at her, and he knew she was wondering what she could do to escape from Mr. Howell now that he had prevented her from drowning.

"Why did you not trust me?" the Duke asked. "Surely you realised that, once I knew who you were and saw how unpleasant that swine was who was frightening you, I would save you?"

"But how can . . . you . . . without becoming . . . involved?" Helga asked. "He is evil and . . . vindictive, and would damage your . . . reputation and . . . enjoy doing so."

"You must think me very weak and resourceless if you do not trust me," the Duke said.

"I want to . . . you know I want to," Helga replied, "and you are so . . . magnificent that I feel you could do anything . . . but this is an impossible . . . problem for you to solve . . . and nothing can be done, except that I . . . m-marry Mr. Howell . . . as he wants me to."

The Duke heard the terror in her voice and felt her whole body shiver against his and he said:

"That is something which I swear to you will never happen, and you are not to think of it again."

"But . . . he will compel me!" Helga insisted. "How can I . . . escape him?"

"That is what I am going to tell you," the Duke said, "but first I want to ask you something."

She looked up at him, then as if she were suddenly conscious of her wet cheeks she rubbed at them with the knuckles of her hand as a child might have done.

There was something in the movement which the Duke found very endearing.

"What do you . . . want to . . . ask me?"

He knew she was making a tremendous effort to be calm and to speak naturally.

"I want to know exactly what you feel about me as a man," the Duke said.

He saw Helga's eyes widen with surprise at the question. Then she said:

"I think you are magnificent and very impressive as a Duke. As a man, you are kind and understanding, and as I know, very . . . perceptive, and perhaps you will think it a strange word, but you are also very . . . sensitive."

The Duke knew she was considering him clairvoyantly, and he said:

"Thank you, Helga, but I want to know more. I want to know what you personally feel about me."

Helga drew in her breath.

"I am very . . . grateful to you . . . because you have been so . . . kind to me."

"Nothing more?"

"I . . . I do not . . . understand."

"I was thinking of what Milly told you not to feel about me," the Duke said.

"That I . . . love you?" Helga asked in a voice that was hardly audible. "Of course I . . . love you! How could I help . . . it? But I would not be a . . . nuisance or . . . an embarrassment . . . It is just that as one cannot help . . . loving the sun . . . the flowers and the moonlight I love you."

"As I love you!" the Duke said very quietly.

He bent his head to find her lips.

For a second Helga could not believe it was actually happening.

Then as the Duke's kiss held her captive she knew that she loved him overwhelmingly with her heart and soul exactly in the way her aunt had warned her she must not do.

But how could she help it when he was so irresistible, everything she had dreamt of and longed to find in a man?

At the same time he was so very human and understanding in the same way as her instinct taught her how to feel.

'I love him! I love him!' she thought as he kissed her.

Then as if the moonlight had seeped from outside into her body, she felt the shafts of it moving up into her breasts through her throat and onto her lips.

It was so ecstatic, so spiritual, so much a part of the mystical world she had known since a child, that the Duke suddenly filled the whole world and he was also in a strange way part of her prayers and her belief in God.

Only as he raised his head did she manage to say incoherently:

"I . . . love you . . . I love you . . . and I never knew . . . anything could be so wonderful . . . so perfect as you!"

"My precious!" the Duke said. "That is what I should be saying to you!"

Then he was kissing her again, kissing her with long, slow passionate kisses that drew her heart and her soul from her body and they were no longer hers, but his.

It was a long time later before the Duke said vaguely,

as if he were only just aware of what they were doing:

"We cannot stay out here all night. I must take you back."

"I feel as if I have ... died and am in ... Heaven!" Helga whispered.

The rapture in her voice and the expression in her eyes made the Duke draw in his breath.

He knew that many women had loved him, but Helga's love was different, and he understood that she had been swept away by an ecstasy that was part of the Divine.

"How can I have been so unbelievably lucky as to have found you?" he asked.

He drew her back through the orchard and into the garden.

Only as they reached the shadows of the house did Helga ask in a frightened little voice:

"What is ... going to ... happen to me?"

The Duke put his arms around her again.

"You are going to stay with me," he said. "I am going to look after you and protect you, not, my precious, in the way I suggested before, but as my wife!"

He felt Helga stiffen and realised that not for one moment had the idea of marriage crossed her mind.

Then as he waited she asked:

"Did you really say ... as your ... wife?"

"It is your own fault that I did not realise it sooner," the Duke said, "for trying to deceive me into believing you were an actress pretending to be a Lady. I know now, my precious, that you are what I have always been looking for but never found: someone who loves me for myself and whom I love because she is everything I want and need to be with me for the rest of my life."

Helga drew in her breath and he added gently:

"You said you love me as a man."

"I adore you ... I worship you," Helga said, "but I think perhaps it would be ... wrong for me to ... m-marry you."

"Why should it be wrong?"

"Because I am not ... clever enough and I know so very ... little about the world in which ... you live. Supposing after you ... marry me you become ... bored and decide ... you have made a ... mistake?"

The Duke laughed and it was a very happy sound.

"You are perceptive," he said, "and you have admitted that I am too. I know with my perception, just as you know with yours, that we shall be marvellously happy, so much so that the whole world, although they do not matter, will be surprised."

"Are you sure ... absolutely ... sure?"

"Let me ask you the same question," the Duke replied. "Are you sure you would be happy with me?"

She drew in her breath and looked at him, needing no words to tell him what she was feeling. Then she said:

"It is such a wonderful idea ... but I feel it ... cannot be true."

"It is true!" the Duke said. "And now, my darling, all you have to do is to leave everything to me, and you need never be frightened again."

"But I am frightened ... frightened that ... something might ... hurt you."

"I can look after myself, and you," the Duke said. "All you have to do, my sweet, is to believe me."

He looked down at her in the moonlight, but he did

not kiss her, his lips only resting for a moment against her forehead.

Then he drew her towards the door he had left open which led into the house.

They went up the side staircase and the Duke took her to her Bedroom and when they reached it he said:

"I want you to go to sleep and think only of our love and how happy we are going to be together."

He looked at her in the light of the candle that was burning beside the bed.

"Do you swear to me on everything you hold sacred that you will not, when I leave you, do anything so foolish as to try to run away or to harm yourself?"

Helga put out her hands towards him.

"I . . . promise," she said, "and . . . promise me you are sure . . . you are doing the right thing . . . and that people will not be . . . shocked, and it will not . . . hurt you."

"The only thing that could hurt me now," the Duke said, "is if I lost you. You are everything in my life, Helga, and that is why you have to promise me that there will be no more dramatics, nothing that will make me afraid."

"I . . . promise!"

She lifted her face to his like a child, and the Duke kissed her.

Then very gently he took off her negligee and lifted her into bed, pulling the sheets up to her chin before he said:

"Go to sleep, Helga. I shall give orders that you are not to be called until you awaken, and by the time you do I will have everything arranged."

As he spoke he realised that Helga was hardly listening

but looking at him with an expression of love and adoration in her eyes which made him feel almost as if she were kneeling in front of him and treating him as if he were a Saint.

Very tenderly he kissed her.

Before he blew out the light beside the bed he said:

"I know your mother was looking after you and protecting you tonight when I came in search of you, and she will protect you until morning."

As he spoke he knew it was a very strange thing for him to think of saying.

Then he left Helga in the darkness, realising that in some extraordinary way she had already changed his life and his thinking, and would continue to do so.

* * *

The Duke was in his Study in the morning when the door opened and Helga came in.

For a moment she just stood looking at him from across the room, and he knew she was feeling shy and a little uncertain of herself.

He had been waiting to see her, and when she was there he felt his whole body leap into an alertness at her presence that brought him to his feet. Then he just held out his arms.

He saw her eyes widen with excitement. Then she ran towards him and as he held her close against him she asked:

"Is it true . . . really true what . . . happened last night? I thought perhaps it had . . . just been a . . . dream."

"It is true that I love you."

"I . . . I can hardly . . . believe it!"

The rapture of her tone made the Duke hold her close before he kissed her.

Then as his lips found hers it was a gentle kiss, as if he dedicated himself to her service.

Then he said almost briskly, as if he pulled himself to attention:

"If you are ready, my dearest, we must leave for London."

"For . . . London?" Helga asked, a little tremor in her voice. "But . . . I thought . . ."

He knew she was thinking that at four o'clock Bernard Howell would be calling for her at Grosvenor Square.

"Everything has been planned and you promised to trust me."

"I do trust you . . . but . . ."

"There are no 'buts,'" he interrupted, "and there is no need to be frightened."

He smiled and it illuminated his face before he said:

"There is only one thing I want to do, and that is to escape from here before what remains of my house party is aware that we have left."

Without his saying so, Helga knew he was thinking of the Countess of Carrington, and she said quickly:

"Can we do . . . that?"

"I told you, everything is arranged," the Duke said. "All you have to do is put on your bonnet and cape, which you will find waiting for you on the chair over there, then we are going to slip out through one of the back doors, where my Chaise is waiting for us."

Helga gave a little laugh.

"It sounds very exciting!"

"Everything we do from now on will be, you will find, very exciting," the Duke replied, "and different from anything either of us has ever done in the past."

She put on the small bonnet which tied under her chin, then the Duke put her travelling cape over her shoulders, his hands lingering for a moment against her neck.

Then taking her by the hand he hurried her down the passage away from the Main Hall, and as he had said outside another door which was rarely used was waiting his Chaise drawn by a team of four perfectly matched horses.

There was no one to see them off, only a groom who handed the reins to the Duke, then climbed up behind.

They drove off and only when they were some way away from Rock did Helga ask:

"What will everybody think when they find you gone?"

"I have left a very plausible explanation for my absence with my secretary," the Duke replied. "Now, forget the past, Helga, we are stepping into the future, you and I, and as I promised you, it will be very exciting!"

They reached London in record time, and as they swept up to the front door of the big house in Grosvenor Square, Helga could not help feeling a little apprehensively that in a few hours Bernard Howell would be arriving and, if nothing else, there would be an unpleasant scene which would spoil the happiness she was feeling with the Duke.

She did not say anything and as he helped her out of the Chaise and up the steps to the front door, he said:

"I expect you would like to tidy yourself. You will find the maids are waiting for you in the room upstairs."

There was a Housekeeper in rustling black silk, the

154

silver chatelaine at her waist, to show Helga the way.

She was shown into a magnificent Bedroom over-looking the Square, where she found two maids waiting to help her change from her travelling clothes into one of the prettiest of the white gowns which she had taken with her to Rock.

She did not need to ask how it had managed to get there so quickly because when she had woken up that morning she realised that the maids were packing her trunk.

She remembered seeing it being taken from her room before she had gone downstairs to find the Duke.

She guessed it had been brought to London by train which was the only way they could have travelled more swiftly than she and the Duke had managed to do in the Chaise.

Because there was a rising excitement within her she did not ask any questions, but when she was dressed in the white gown which was very becoming she looked at herself in the mirror and prayed that he would think her pretty and go on loving her.

There was a footman to take her down the stairs and she found the Duke in what she felt was his special room because the walls were lined with books.

He was waiting for her, and she saw that he too had changed from the clothes in which he had travelled from Rock into more conventional town clothes.

As soon as the footman had shut the door behind him she ran towards him eagerly.

"You have been quick, my lovely one," he said, "which is a good thing, because we have a lot to do."

She looked at him questioningly and he said quietly:

"The first thing is to be married!"

"M-married . . . now . . . today?"

"As soon as we reach the Grosvenor Chapel."

It seemed as if a thousand lights had been turned on in Helga's eyes.

She put out both her hands towards the Duke as if to make sure he was really there and she was not dreaming.

"You will understand that it has to be a quiet wedding," the Duke said, "a secret ceremony for which I have obtained a Special Licence. It would be difficult for one thing to explain to Mr. Vanderfeld that I did not marry Miss Helga Grosvenor, but the Honourable Helga Wensley."

He laughed before he went on:

"For another, I want to make you my wife and tell you how much I love you before we listen to the congratulations and also the astonishment of our friends."

"It sounds very . . . very . . . wonderful!" Helga cried.

"Then we will go to Grosvenor Chapel immediately," the Duke said, "and as I would not wish you to be disappointed, my darling, because you cannot wear the conventional veil and diamond tiara that is usually worn by the Duchesses of Rocklington, I have brought you a wreath of white orchids which will appear to anyone who sees it just an ordinary piece of headgear, but to you and me it will mean something very different."

He took the wreath as he spoke from where it was lying on the chair and placed it carefully on her head.

It made Helga look, he thought, even younger and more springlike than she had before, and after a long moment he asked:

"Could anyone be lovelier?"

Then once again they were driving through the streets, but this time in a closed carriage.

On the small seat beside them was a box and the Duke took from it a small bouquet made of the same white orchids that Helga wore on her head.

"For my bride!" he said.

"Now I really feel like one," Helga answered.

Then as the horses came to a standstill, for the Grosvenor Chapel was only a very short distance from Rocklington House, she said:

"You know how . . . marvellous this is for me . . . but are you quite certain you will not be . . . sorry that you married . . . me?"

"I am quite, quite certain, that this is the best thing I have ever done in my whole life!" the Duke answered.

He saw the tears of happiness come into Helga's eyes and he kissed her hand before he took her up the steps and through the porticoed door of the Grosvenor Chapel which had seen so many secret marriages since it was first built in 1730.

A Parson was waiting for them at the altar, and as Helga went up the aisle on the Duke's arm, she felt as if the Church were not empty, but filled with the songs of angels and a happiness that enveloped them both like a cloud of glory.

The Duke made his responses in a firm voice, almost as if he had fought a battle to win her, and was determined to make sure of his conquest.

Helga's voice was low, and yet she felt as if her whole being vibrated towards the man beside her, and that even before the ring was on her finger and the Priest had blessed them they were not two people but one.

As they drove away from the Grosvenor Chapel the Duke said:

"Now that you are my wife, my darling, we are eloping."

"Eloping?" Helga asked in astonishment.

"I know that like me you will have no wish to spoil the happiest day of our lives with rows, scenes, recriminations, and above all boring explanations. So we are running away!"

Helga gave a little gasp.

"Where to?"

"Not very far," the Duke replied, "because, as you know, I have to be in touch with Mr. Vanderfeld tomorrow, otherwise his contract will not be signed, and I will not be able to prove your instinct is right and the man Potter is a crook."

Helga gave a little laugh and said:

"You will know I am right because you will use your instinct."

"On Thursday," the Duke went on, "Mr. Vanderfeld goes back to America. Then I intend, my precious darling, to take you to Paris."

"To Paris!" Helga breathed.

"First to buy your trousseau," he said, "because the Countess of Rocklington cannot continue to wear clothes borrowed from the Gaiety Theatre!"

There was a hint of laughter in the Duke's voice as he added:

"Nobody would believe it, but fortunately they will

never know. And to finish my story, after Paris we will go to the South of France, where I have a Villa."

"It sounds too wonderful!" Helga breathed. "But where are we going now?"

"Our hiding place is a house I have in Hampstead which belonged to my grandmother and is a Museum of treasures which I have never had time myself to examine. But we will look at them together when I am not telling you how much I love you."

"How can you think of anything so exciting?" Helga whispered.

She hesitated, then she said in a very small voice:

"And when . . . Mr. Howell calls for me . . . this afternoon?"

"He will be informed by my secretary that I have been obliged to extend your contract of employment with me for another week," the Duke replied. "He may be angry, but there is nothing he can do about it, and in a week's time, when we are far away across the Channel, it will be announced that our marriage has taken place very quietly. It will be impossible then for Howell or your stepfather to interfere or frighten you, my precious, by making a scene."

Helga put her head against the Duke's shoulder.

"How can you have thought of anything so brilliant?" she asked.

"I am glad you think it a rather clever arrangement," the Duke replied. "The one thing I have always dreaded is an elaborate wedding ceremony with crowds of people filling St. George's Hanover Square and a huge reception at which one has to listen to embarrassing speeches."

Helga laughed.

"There is no one to make any speeches now except yourself."

"I shall have a great deal to say, and although my audience will be a small one, I feel she will listen."

"I love you!" Helga said. "You are not only clever and very, very exciting, but also so full of surprises that I feel as if you are a magic Conjurer!"

"The magic is yours," the Duke said, "but I think we will bewilder and bemuse those who want to make trouble for us, and pleasantly surprise those who are fond of us."

Helga gave a little cry.

"Aunt Millicent!"

"I have thought of her," the Duke said, "and I have already sent her a letter saying that you will be staying with me for a little longer than we arranged, and we will explain it more fully in a few days' time."

"You think of everything!" Helga said again.

"I am thinking of everything because I am trying to prevent you from worrying or being unhappy and afraid," he said. "And as there is now no reason for any of that, you can spend your time thinking only about me!"

"As if I could do anything else!" Helga cried, and moved a little closer to him.

*   *   *

Later that night in a large Bedroom overlooking the garden filled with ancient trees and a profusion of flowers Helga whispered against the Duke's shoulder:

"I have not . . . disappointed you?"

He pulled her a little closer to him before he said:

"How can you ask such absurd questions? I have never, my darling, in my whole life known such happiness."

"Is . . . that true?"

"I think you would know if I was lying," the Duke said, "and I swear to you, my lovely one, that I had no idea until tonight that love could be so perfect or so different from anything I have ever known before."

"How can you say anything so wonderful?" Helga asked. "I have been so . . . afraid that you would . . . compare me to the . . . lovely Ladies to whom you have . . . made love and find . . ."

"I find you very young, very innocent, and so exciting," the Duke interrupted, "and I find also that I did not know I was capable of feeling the sensations you arouse in me."

"I thought that you carried me up to Heaven," Helga said, "and it was so utterly and completely marvellous that I must have . . . died because no one could . . . feel as you have made me feel and . . . still be on . . . earth."

She spoke in a rapt little voice that thrilled the Duke and at the same time made him aware that she was different from any other woman he had ever known.

He was experienced enough to know that he must be very gentle and very controlled so as not to frighten her, but because she loved him so overwhelmingly he had found that everything he did seemed to them both to be part of the Divine.

There was a spirituality about their lovemaking which the Duke found so moving and so perfect that he knew that he was not only the teacher, but the pupil.

"I love you! God, how I love you!" he said.

Helga lifted her eyes to his and answered:

"Nobody knows where we are, and I feel we have escaped from the world into a tiny Planet which to everybody else is just a star in the sky."

"That is what I too feel," the Duke agreed, "and there are so many other stars I want to show you, so many other houses I own in different parts of England and abroad also, that we are going to have a very long honeymoon, my darling heart, before you and I come back to work at all the duties and responsibilities that are waiting for us."

"That is what . . . frightens me," Helga said. "Suppose I . . . fail you . . . and you wish you had married somebody who could do things . . . better than I can?"

"That would be impossible."

"Why do . . . you say . . . that?"

"Because, my darling, you bring love and your perception in everything you do and that is what makes you different from other women, especially where it concerns me!"

"How could I do anything but . . . love you?" Helga asked. "I never . . . thought or dreamt when I first went to Rock, and Aunt Millicent warned me against . . . falling in love with you that I should ever be . . . your wife."

"And I was not going to marry anybody," the Duke laughed, "not for many, many years!"

"I think we forgot that . . . God knows best," Helga said, "and brought us together in a very strange way."

"Very strange indeed!" the Duke agreed. "I never expected I would find my wife in the Gaiety Theatre!"

Helga gave a little cry.

"Do you realise if I had not run away from Bernard

Howell and begged Aunt Millicent to help me I would never have met you?"

"I really believe," the Duke said quietly, "that a Power greater than ourselves has been guiding us, protecting us, and giving us the happiness we have now found together."

Helga put her arm round his neck.

"Please, darling," she said, "teach me how to make you happy. Teach me how to love you the way you want to be loved so that you will never . . . never be . . . sorry that you married . . . somebody so unimportant and . . . who was . . . pretending to be . . . an actress."

The Duke laughed.

"I thought I was engaging an actress pretending to be a Lady. How could I have possibly known that instead I had engaged a Lady who was pretending to be an actress?"

"It does seem foolish," Helga said, "and now you have to teach her, and it may be difficult, how to . . . act the . . . part of a . . . Duchess."

"It will not be difficult," the Duke said, "because I shall be looking after you, taking care of you, and teaching you, my darling, how to love the Duke."

"I do that . . . already!"

"Not half as much as I intend to make you love me."

His arms tightened around her before he said:

"I want you to love me with every breath you draw, Helga, with every thought in your adorable head. I shall be jealous of anything you do and anything you think that does not concern me. You are mine, and so infinitely precious and different from anyone else in the world that

I am prepared to go down on my knees and thank God that I have found you."

The sincerity in the way the Duke spoke was very moving and Helga could only say:

"I love you . . . I love you! There are no other words in which to tell you what I feel and . . . how perfect everything is because you are here . . . you are you . . . and you love . . . me!"

There were no words, and as the Duke held her lips captive and his heart beat against hers they were once again swept away on the star on which they were hiding, up into the Heavens.

There they found the perfect love that is both pure and Divine.

ABOUT THE AUTHOR

Barbara Cartland, the world's most famous romantic novelist, who is also an historian, playwright, lecturer, political speaker and television personality, has now written over 400 books and sold over 390 million books the world over.

She has also had many historical works published and has written four autobiographies as well as the biographies of her mother and that of her brother, Ronald Cartland, who was the first Member of Parliament to be killed in the last war. This book has a preface by Sir Winston Churchill and has just been republished with an introduction by Sir Arthur Bryant.

Love at the Helm, a novel written with the help and inspiration of the late Admiral of the Fleet, the Earl Mountbatten of Burma, is being sold for the Mountbatten Memorial Trust.

Miss Cartland in 1978 sang an Album of Love Songs with the Royal Philharmonic Orchestra.

In 1976 by writing twenty-one books, she broke the world record and has continued for the following seven years with twenty-four, twenty, twenty-three, twenty-four, twenty-four, twenty-five, and twenty-three. She is in the *Guinness Book of Records* as the best-selling author in the world.

She is unique in that she was one and two in the Dalton List of Best Sellers, and one week had four books in the top twenty.

In private life Barbara Cartland, who is a Dame of the Order of St. John of Jerusalem, Chairman of the St. John Council in Hertfordshire and Deputy President of the St. John Ambulance Brigade, has also fought for better conditions and salaries for Midwives and Nurses.

Barbara Cartland is deeply interested in Vitamin Therapy and is President of the British National Association for Health. Her book *The Magic of Honey* has sold throughout the world and is translated into many languages. Her designs "Decorating with Love" are being sold all over the U.S.A., and the National Home Fashions League named her in 1981, "Woman of Achievement."

In 1984 she received at Kennedy Airport America's Bishop Wright Air Industry Award for her contribution to the development of aviation; in 1931 she and two R.A.F. Officers thought of, and carried, the first aeroplane-towed glider air-mail.

Barbara Cartland's Romances (a book of cartoons) has been published in Great Britain and the U.S.A., as well as a cookery book, *The Romance of Food*, and *Getting Older, Growing Younger*. She has recently written a children's pop-up picture book, entitled *Princess to the Rescue*.

More romance from
BARBARA CARTLAND

BARBARA CARTLAND

Called after her own
beloved Camfield Place,
each Camfield novel of love
by Barbara Cartland
is a thrilling, never-before published
love story by the greatest romance
writer of all time.

March '86...SAFE AT LAST
April '86...HAUNTED